With a quick flicker
of her eyes, Jessie decided
she could risk moving again.

Just as she stood, the rifle barked once more. Abandoning caution, she lunged ahead. She'd taken only one step when the hush that had settled down following the shot was broken by the metallic clicking of a shell being loaded into a rifle. Jessie moved forward another quick step. As her movement rustled the brush, a man turned, swinging the gun's muzzle toward her.

Jessie shot from the hip, and at such close range there was no way that a marksman of her skill and training could miss. Man and rifle hit the ground at the same time . . .

— • → WESLEY ELLIS ← • —

LONE STAR

AND THE
TOMBSTONE GAMBLE

J®

A JOVE BOOK

LONE STAR AND THE TOMBSTONE GAMBLE

A Jove Book/published by arrangement with
the author

PRINTING HISTORY
Jove edition/February 1986

ISBN: 0-515-08462-X

LONE STAR

AND THE
TOMBSTONE GAMBLE

Chapter 1

"It can't be alkali water that killed them steers, Jessie," Ed Wright complained. "I been in this part of Texas long enough to know that, without even seeing the tank."

Nodding agreement with the Circle Star foreman, Jessie said, "Of course, it's not alkali water, Ed. That's one problem we've never had here."

"Well, there was surely a dozen dead critters lying around the tank," Wright went on. "Fresh dead, too, or so Sam Beard said. At least they hadn't begun bloating."

"I don't suppose Sam stayed there long enough to look at them closely."

Wright shook his head. "He said he figured the best thing for him to do was get back here quick as he could and tell me about 'em. There wasn't any reason for him to stay there; whoever poisoned that water was long gone."

"Yes," Jessie agreed. "He couldn't have done anything if he'd stayed there."

"So it goes back to what I told you at first," Wright said. "Somebody's put poison in that tank, and there's no way of telling how many more he's dosed."

"I suppose you've sent some of the men out to check the others?" Jessie asked.

"Oh, sure," Wright replied. "That was the first thing I did, even before I came here to tell you about the dead steers that Sam found. Before the day's out, we'll know if the other tanks have been poisoned."

Ki spoke for the first time. "I feel the way Jessie does, Ed. It's certain to be poison. Alex made sure there wouldn't be any alkali water problems. I was with him when he checked that south range before he bought it. There were only three tanks on it then and two or three natural waterholes that weren't much more than puddles—not nearly enough water to carry the number of cattle he was planning to put in."

"I remember going to the south range with Alex when I was just, oh, about ten years old," Jessie said. "He'd hired some laborers from the railroad gangs to make tanks out of the waterholes." She hesitated for a moment, her eyes growing sad at the memory of her adored father, who was murdered by the cartel's gunmen. "I'd never really seen men working so hard before, digging that ground near the spring and piling the dirt around the edge. I guess that's why I remember it so well."

"You were still at school when Alex really began to develop the south range," Ki said to Jessie. "I saw Alex pick up a shovel and dig shoulder to shoulder with the hands. He'd hold his own with them, too."

Ed Wright had remained silent during the few moments in which Jessie and Ki recalled the past. Now, he broke in and asked, "I guess you'll want to go see what Sam Beard found out there by that tank, Jessie?"

"Of course, I will, Ed. Let me know as soon as you get a report from the men who're checking the other tanks. Ki and I will be ready to ride out there with you."

Wright stood up. "I'll stop at the cookhouse and tell Gimpy to have something ready for us to eat and fix us some sandwiches to take along. It's not likely we'll be back in time for supper."

"No," Ki agreed. He said nothing more until Wright had left, and then he went on, "I'm sure you're thinking the same thing I am, Jessie."

2

"Of course," she said, "the cartel. They're getting more and more aggressive, Ki."

"My guess is that they've gotten some new leadership," Ki said slowly, "men who're trying to impress the old bosses."

"I'm sure you're right, Ki," Jessie answered. "We've seen that happen before, of course — like the time they made that mass attack on the Circle Star and . . ."

Jessie's voice faltered and she fell silent. Ki said nothing; he understood Jessie's moods as an older brother might know the reactions of a younger sister. He could see that Jessie was now in the grip of the sorrow she always felt when she recalled Alex Starbuck's death in a shower of bullets from the cartel's hired assassins, but he knew that her mood would change quickly when the time came for action.

As a youth, Ki had joined Alex. His mother had been cast out of her family after eloping with the American businessman who was Ki's father. Bitter because of the action of his grandparents, blaming his father for his mother's early death, Ki had spent his youth as a drifter, moving from place to place in the orient. His longest stay had been on the island of Okinawa, where he learned the art of weaponless combat.

Arriving in the United States, angry and friendless, Ki had gone to the only American he knew, Alex Starbuck, looking for a job. Alex employed Ki without question, and as the years passed Ki became his right-hand man.

Understanding Jessie's moods, Ki knew when her silence continued that she needed solitude for a while, and said, "I think it would be a good idea for me to go and talk with Sam Beard. He might remember more about what he saw and that might give us a clue."

Jessie nodded silently. After Ki had gone, she sat motionless in the big leather armchair in the room that had been Alex's study, her mind still on the past.

Until he died, Alex had been the most active American

3

enemy of the sinister cartel. Ironically, it was Alex's business success that had first brought him into contact with the cartel, for in his own lifetime Alex Starbuck had become a legendary figure.

From his modest beginning, a small import house that he'd started in San Francisco with an investment of only a few hundred dollars, Alex had rather quickly become a tycoon. The success of his importing operation had enabled him to buy a battered freighter to bring his own cargo across the Pacific from the Orient.

When he lacked enough merchandise to fill the sturdy old ship's hold, Alex had begun soliciting cargo from others who imported goods from Asia. Rather than having his single vessel cross the Pacific empty on its return trip, he'd aggressively hunted cargo from friends and acquaintances he'd made through his growing business network.

Within a few years his success had enabled him to expand his one aging freighter into a shipping line. By the time his operations were running smoothly, iron-hulled ships were beginning to replace those of wood. Alex had judged correctly that within a few years the new kind of ships would make obsolete the vulnerable wooden vessels. He tried to buy new ships to replace the aging craft of his small fleet, but others had also seen the implications of the new technology, and he faced a long waiting line.

Instead of waiting to invest his funds in ships, Alex established a foundry to produce iron plates and a small shipyard to fabricate the vessels he needed. This venture was even more successful than his shipping line. Owning the foundry and shipyard quickly led Alex into iron mining, from which he soon branched out into copper, gold, and silver mines.

Exasperated by the caution of timid bankers who'd been reluctant to finance him, Starbuck founded a small bank and expanded the bank into a major financial institution.

While he was still relatively young, Alex drew the attention of key men in banking and other financial enterprises.

Before he was forty, Alex was a millionaire many times over and his individual holdings had been widely expanded. In addition to his shipping line and the mines he owned, he'd acquired stands of timber as well as lumber mills. He'd bought stock in other enterprises and had been invited to join the boards of directors of railroads, banks, and a brokerage house.

His success had also drawn the eyes of industrialists in Europe, especially those of a group of unscrupulous financiers, factory owners, and petty nobility. A half century earlier, this group had formed a cartel to bring control of Europe's key business and industries into their hands. Having successfully ensnared enough firms in Europe and Asia to ensure the success of their project, the cartel's members began looking greedily at the United States and had started to nibble their way into American industry.

Mistakenly judging that as a newcomer to the list of America's industrial giants Alex would welcome a short cut to the top of the heap, the cartel tried to enlist them as a member. Alex had been outraged. He informed the representatives who'd approached him that he would fight to defeat the cartel's schemes.

In spite of his success, Alex Starbuck had remained modest and unassuming. He married late, a marriage that became only a tragic memory when his beloved young wife died. Alex treasured Jessie as his living reminder of her mother.

At the time of his wife's death, Alex had just bought a faltering cattle ranch in southwest Texas and renamed it the Circle Star. To keep his mind from dwelling on the tragedy that had befallen him, he turned his energies to finishing the home he'd started on the ranch. The arid area somehow matched his spirits at the moment, and Alex came to love the ranch, to consider it his home. Even before the big house on the Circle Star was fully completed, Alex had made the ranch his home.

Jessie had grown up there, attended in infancy and early childhood by a wise old geisha whom Alex had met early in his business career in the Orient. Later, Ki helped the old woman look after Jessie when he and Alex were not traveling. After Alex's murder, Ki had stayed on and served Jessie with the same loyalty he'd given her father.

At last, Jessie's unhappy thoughts faded and vanished; her mind returned to the problem of the poisoned waterhole. She went upstairs to her bedroom, took her Colt from the drawer of her bedside table, and sat down to clean it.

Ki found Sam Beard in the horse corral, grooming his pony. "Figured I better take a look at him," the cowhand said. "I pushed him pretty good on the way back here from that tank, and he had a swallow or two of that poison water before I tumbled on to what was wrong."

"You're sure it was the water that killed those steers?" Ki asked. "Did you look at them to see if they'd been shot?"

"I just looked at one," Beard replied. "Seeing the carcasses sprawled all around the tank when I rode up got me sorta boogery. I swung down from my saddle to get a closer look at the first one I came to, and while I was bending down trying to see if the critter'd been shot, my pony wandered to the tank. Lucky I noticed him right away and yelled for him to come back, but he was at the water by then."

"Was he drinking?"

"Just starting to. I don't guess he could've put down more'n a swallow before I got to him, though."

"He looks all right," Ki said, scanning the compact pony. "And if he drank enough of the water to hurt him, he'd be acting sick by now."

"I reckon," Beard said. "But I tell you, that waterhole ain't a pretty sight. Eleven steers down and two more stag-

6

gering like they was about to drop any minute."

"Was there anything else dead around the tank, Sam?"

Shaking his head, the cowpoke answered, "I didn't notice anything. Course, I wasn't looking close, but I reckon if a dead coyote or a badger or something like that had been lying around I'd've seen it."

Ki nodded and then asked, "What about the main herd on that south range?"

"Oh, I lucked out on it. When I was on my way back here I saw the herd making for the waterhole. I figured it was best for me to take care of the steers, so I turned the critters away from the tank. It'll take 'em the rest of the day to get back to it."

"I don't suppose you had time to do any scouting at the tank, looking for the tracks of whoever poisoned it?"

"Hell's bells, Ki!" Beard protested. "I had my plate full just trying to figure out what killed the steers and worrying about my pony and then moving that south range herd as far from that poisoned water as I could move 'em!"

"Of course, you did," Ki agreed. "And you did the right thing. I'll be sure to tell Jessie about the cattle you saved by moving the herd away from the tank."

"Well, now, I wasn't doing nothing special, just what I draw wages for. But thanks, Ki."

Ki started back toward the main house, but before reaching it he met Jessie on her way to the corral. She was carrying her saddlebags and rifle.

"Are you getting ready to go now?" he asked.

"I've got an idea," Jessie replied, "but before we talk about it, tell me what you learned from Sam."

"He told me a few bits and pieces that Ed hadn't mentioned, but the only important thing he said was that he'd chased the south range herd as far from the poisoned water as he could."

"We can depend on Ed to handle the cattle, Ki," Jessie

replied. "But I think we'd better start out for that poisoned tank as soon as the man Ed sent to the nearest one to it gets back."

Ki got Jessie's point at once. "Of course. The next tank to the one on the south range would tell us whether the poisoner had covered more of them."

"And Ed can take care of things, either way." Jessie nodded. "I want to get to the tank we know about and see what we can find out."

"Ed said he'd have Gimpy get some lunches together for us," Ki told her. "Why don't you saddle up while I find out if he has a couple of them ready? If he hasn't, he can put them together while I get my rifle and a *shuriken*, and we'll be on our way as soon as I saddle a horse."

Jessie rode Sun. The palomino's long easy strides ate up space while Ki tried to keep his roan mare abreast, and they reached the tank in little more than an hour. Even before they got to the foot of the long rise that led to the poisoned tank, they saw the buzzards circling it.

Exchanging glances and nods when they saw the scavengers, they touched their horses' flanks with their heels and speeded steadily up the slope until they reached the crest. The tank was only a short distance away, a rough circle created on the level prairie by shoveling earth away from the spring that fed it.

They could not see the water yet, only the low bank that confined it. For fifty yards around the tank, the yellow soil had been beaten bare by hooves and on the pocked earth the carcasses of the poisoned cattle lay scattered. As Jessie and Ki drew closer, the five or six buzzards that had been ripping at the carcasses were waddling away from their meal.

As they retreated, the big black birds spread their wings

8

and began flapping. By the time Jessie and Ki reached the foot of the hump, the buzzards had risen from the ground and were gaining altitude with every stroke of their powerful wings.

"Sam Beard said he'd counted eleven steers down and two more staggering," Ki said. "There are thirteen carcasses lying around here now, so I guess those two died after he'd started back."

"Sam must have gotten here just a little while after the poisoner had gone, then." Jessie frowned. "We don't need to waste our time examining those carcasses, Ki. Suppose we circle around the tank and see if we can pick up his trail."

Dismounting, they began walking slowly around the tank's perimeter, their eyes searching the moist soil at the water's edge. They'd gone halfway around the tank when they discovered what they were looking for, imprints of range boots in the moist soil at the water's edge.

"That's where he squatted down to toss the poison in," Ki said. "Look how deep the toes of his boots dug in when he leaned forward."

"I'd certainly like to know what kind of poison he used," Jessie stated. "If we know that and find that he's poisoned the other tanks, we will be able to neutralize it. I'd hate to keep losing steers for the next few months."

"We'd better put off thinking about that until we know just how badly we've been hit," Ki suggested. "Right now, I'm more interested in seeing if he left a trail we can follow."

"Yes, of course," Jessie agreed. She looked along the rim of the tank and pointed to a series of oval patches leading away from the tank. "There's where the topsoil stuck to his wet bootsoles when he left the tank. At least we can follow him to where he left his horse."

Ki joined Jessie and they followed the oval marks to a

9

short distance from the tank, where a heap of fresh manure marked the place where the poisoner's horse had stood waiting. Ki hunkered down and started peering at the hard soil, his head close to the ground. Jessie leaned forward and began her own examination. Ki shifted his position and she followed him.

"It'll be slow going, but we can trail him, all right," Ki said after a moment or two. "His horse must've thrown the shoe off its right, front hoof. See here."

Looking where Ki was pointing, Jessie saw three sets of the triangular dents. The fourth hoofprint was a plain U-shaped curve.

"It's lucky the grass hasn't come up on this part of the range yet," she commented. "The ground's still bare enough for tracks to show through it."

"Just what I was thinking," Ki said. "If you'll lead my horse for a few minutes, I'll follow these tracks on foot until we can be sure which way that fellow went."

Ki started following the tracks, bending close to the ground, slowing down occasionally when the marks disappeared on an unusually hard or thick, grassy spot. In such places he was forced to cast about, zigzagging until he was sure he'd picked up the right set of prints. The tracks made a semicircle around the tank's perimeter, then led southwest in an almost straight line.

After they'd been moving in the same direction for a while, he stopped, straightened up, and called to Jessie, "I'd say he's heading for the Cross Spikes."

"It does look that way," she agreed. "Do you think it's safe for us to ride for it without worrying about following his tracks?"

"I'm tempted to," Ki replied as she reined over to him and pulled up. "As long as the ground's level, I'm sure I can see the tracks pretty well from the saddle, and if I lose them it'll only take a few minutes for me to pick them up again. But when we reach that little stretch that's all cut up by coulees, I'll have to follow them on foot again."

Moving now at a slow canter, they rode straight ahead, Ki's eyes fixed to the ground. Ki looked up after they'd covered most of the distance to the place where the level prairie gave way to a stretch of shallow coulees.

Jessie anticipated what Ki was going to say. "We'll save a lot of time if we circle the coulees instead of trying to go across them," Jessie suggested. "So far, whoever it is we're after has set a straight line."

"Let's do it, then," Ki agreed. "If we lose the tracks in the coulees, I can always pick—"

Before he could finish, a shot cracked from the area ahead. A rifle bullet plowed into the ground in front of them, kicking up a puff of dust. Before the sniper in the coulees got off a second shot, both Jessie and Ki had hit the ground and flattened out. The next shot from the hidden ambusher cut the air above the backs of their horses and whistled off into space.

Chapter 2

"I don't think we'll have to try to follow that fellow's tracks from here on, Ki," Jessie observed. "My guess is that we've caught up with him."

"More than likely his horse couldn't go any farther," Ki replied. "If you've noticed its hoofprints, it hasn't been putting much weight on that unshod hoof for a while."

"Well, we can be sure of one thing, at least," Jessie went on. "That rider's a stranger to this part of the country. Nobody who knew it would ride into a coulee."

They lay silently, waiting for some indication of movement in the shallow brushy hollows in front of them. What ranchers of the semiarid southwest Texas prairies called coulees were shallow depressions, usually clustered like crisscrossed fingers, perhaps the result of some earthquake that had created a network of cracks in the earth. A few big coulees might cover two or three square miles, but usually the area covered was much smaller, seldom spreading over more than a half mile in width and a mile or so in length.

Over the centuries since the prairie coulees had been formed, erosion had sent dirt down their sides to fill their thin bottoms. This constant process not only gave the coulees a floor, but it widened them and turned their sides from sheer vertical walls into slopes. Some of the gashes in the earth now had bottoms that were only a few feet below the level of the surrounding prairie; others were still deep enough to allow a man on horseback to ride through them with his head well below the prairie.

Because the coulees were the lowest ground on the prairies, they collected rainwater and blowing seeds. Sheltered from the surface wind, brush flourished in them. In some it grew in such thick tangles that a rider could make his way only slowly and with extreme difficulty. Ranchers and cowhands who were familiar with coulees avoided them and circled around them, and the cowhands added new profane words to their vocabulary any time they were forced to go into a coulee when trying to find a stray steer.

Finding a man who was trying to hide in a coulee network was a frustrating experience. Unlike a stray steer, which blundered along crashing through the thick network of interlocking bushes, a man had the sense to remain motionless. Jessie and Ki watched in vain for moving bushes, which would enable them to locate the hidden sniper.

"We can split up and put him in a crossfire," Jessie suggested at last. "But let's try to take him alive. If we can get him to talk, I'm sure he'll be able to answer some of the questions that have been bothering me."

"That's about what I've been thinking," Ki added. "But we'd better take our horses with us and tether them where they'll be out of sight. He might be able to dodge us long enough to get to one; then we'd be in the same jam he is. Which side do you want to take?"

"It doesn't make any difference," she replied. "We can just angle off from here."

Jessie and Ki had faced similar situations so many times in the past that they had no need to make elaborate plans. They moved at once, hugging the ground and leading their horses as they crawled forward. Jessie got a glimpse of Ki as he rose to lead his pony down the coulee wall; then she was at the curving rim herself and had to give all of her

14

attention to making as little noise as possible while she worked Sun through the tangled brush that lined the sides and bottom of the curving depression.

"Stand, Sun," Jessie told the palomino when they reached the bottom of the coulee. She rested her hand reassuringly on Sun's shoulder for a second or two, then reached for the Winchester in her saddle scabbard.

Before her hand touched the rifle, she shook her head and let her arm drop to her side as she realized that the thick brush was likely to deflect its high velocity slugs and cause them to go wild. Then, on second thought, she lifted the Winchester and emptied its magazine before returning it to the leather sheath. She took a careful step away from Sun and stopped to listen.

If the man they were after was between her and Ki, he was not moving. No sounds of rustling bushes reached Jessie's ears as she began working her way along the coulee's bottom. Making a noiseless advance was a slow process. In order to avoid disturbing the thick brush and warning the quarry, she was forced to bend and twist as she picked her way ahead.

She'd moved only a few dozen yards from her starting point when the man in the coulee did what Jessie had successfully avoided doing. She heard a faint rustling close at hand and froze at once. As she strained her ears trying to locate the spot where the sound came from, she slid her Colt from its holster. The thicket in which she stood was almost impenetrable. She could see nothing except dense growth on all sides, and the noise that had alerted her was not repeated.

She started forward again, but before she had moved more than a step or two, the silence was shattered by a rifle blast just ahead. Jessie felt a surge of alarm. Knowing Ki's aversion to firearms, she was sure he had not taken his rifle

15

when he started toward their common goal. Counting on the rifleman's being deafened momentarily by the shot he'd just fired, she pushed on rapidly, ignoring the rustling she made as she fought through the dense growth.

Before she'd advanced more than five or six steps, she saw a flash of motion ahead. Jessie stopped at once. The brush in front of her was still thick, and the small sound she'd heard had given her no clue regarding her distance from the mysterious man she was stalking. As the seconds dragged by, Jessie grew restless. She was positive the shot she'd heard had been aimed at Ki, and the thought that it might have cut him down was picking insistently at her mind.

She took a careful step forward and stopped to listen. Hearing nothing, she moved ahead another step. A whisper of movement came from the brush just ahead and Jessie hunkered down instantly. The undergrowth close to the ground was thinner, and little more than two yards in front of her she saw a booted foot. The toe of the boot was slanted away from her. Jessie studied it with a quick flicker of her eyes and decided she could risk moving again.

Just as she stood, the rifle barked once more. Abandoning caution, Jessie lunged ahead. She'd taken only one step when the hush that had settled down following the shot was broken by the metallic clicking of a shell being loaded into a rifle. Jessie moved forward another quick step. She pulled back when she saw that her advance had brought her to the edge of a tiny clearing. It was barely large enough for the unshaven man who was standing poised, looking away from Jessie, a rifle at his shoulder. As Jessie's movement rustled the brush, he turned, swinging the gun's muzzle toward her.

Jessie's Colt moved faster than the long rifle barrel. She shot from the hip, by instinct, and at such close range there was no way that a marksman of her skill and training could

16

miss. The man's torso jerked as the slug from the Colt went home. The rifle sagged, then fell from his hands. Man and rifle hit the ground at the same time.

In the stillness that followed her shot, Ki called from somewhere beyond the little clearing, "Jessie?"

"I'm here, Ki," she replied.

"Are you all right?"

"Of course. And I got the man we were after."

The bushes ahead of her rustled and moved, and Ki appeared at the edge of the tiny clearing. His eyes flicked over the motionless figure sprawled across the rifle; then he looked up at Jessie.

"I don't suppose you've seen him before?"

Jessie shook her head. "I just got a quick glimpse of his face, Ki. I'm sure I never ran across him."

Ki bent over the body and turned the man's face up. "I haven't either," he told Jessie. "But he's got to have a base of operation near here."

"My guess is the Cross Spikes. He was moving in that direction."

"Let's see if we can find his horse," Ki suggested. "It's got to be pretty close."

Pushing into the brushy tangle, they soon found the mystery man's horse in a deeper coulee a short distance from the spot where he'd been lying in wait for Jessie and Ki. The animal was standing on three legs, a foreleg raised to keep its hoof off the ground. Jessie pointed to the brand on the horse's rump.

"It's a Cross Spikes horse, all right," she said. "But I just can't imagine that Bob Close would be involved in poisoning our steers."

"I'm as sure of that as you are," Ki agreed. "That fellow you brought down probably posed as a drifter and picked up a temporary job there."

17

Ki started walking around the horse. He took a quick look at the hoof it was holding up and told Jessie, "It's thrown a shoe, all right, and when the shoe tore off, it took a big chunk of horn with it. No wonder it's favoring this front hoof. I'd imagine that's why the fellow who poisoned that tank turned back. He was—" Ki stopped abruptly and moved to the animal's saddle.

"What is it, Ki?" Jessie asked.

"There's a flour sack tied to one of the saddle strings," he replied. "I glanced at it and assumed it was his lunch, but now I'm not so sure." As he spoke, Ki untied the sack and glanced into it. He said, "Come take a look, Jessie. We're lucky he made a bad choice when he picked out this horse."

"What're you talking about?" Jessie asked as she moved around the horse to join Ki.

He spread the top of the flour sack open and held it out for her inspection. The bag held a dozen or more smaller white cloth sacks, their mouths closed with yellow draw-strings.

Jessie glanced at the sacks and frowned. "Why would he want to carry so much Bull Durham?"

Ki shook his head. "These are Bull Durham sacks, all right, Jessie, but I'll bet any amount that there's not any tobacco in them."

"Of course!" Jessie said, her eyes widening. "The poison! Why, Ki, there's enough here to poison a dozen tanks!"

"Which is what that fellow was setting out to do." Ki nodded. "If he hadn't picked out a horse with a loose shoe and been forced to turn back, he'd have tossed these sacks into every tank on the Circle Star range before we knew anything about it."

"I'd say we're very lucky!" Jessie said. Then, her voice hardened and she went on, "I almost always feel bad when I'm forced to shoot somebody, Ki. You know that. But this

18

time I don't have a bit of pity for that man lying back there!"

"I don't blame you," Ki agreed. Then he added, "We can be sure now that the cartel's at work again, Jessie."

"No question about it," she said. "And we'd better go on to the Cross Spikes and find out from Bob Close what kind of story the dead man told when Bob hired him."

"He's one of my hands, all right," Bob Close confirmed when he looked at the face of the man Jessie had shot. "Or was, I guess I should say. But all I know about him is his name."

Jessie and Ki had draped the man's body across the saddle of the foot-sore horse and lashed his wrists and ankles together for the slow trip to the main house of Close's spread. Because they'd had to slow the pace of their own mounts to accommodate the lame foot of the animal they were leading, the ride had taken much longer than usual. It had taken them most of the afternoon.

"What did he say his name was?" Ki asked.

"Well, he answered to Jack Bannon, but from what you've said, I have a load of doubt that's his name," Close told her.

"Do you mind telling me what he was supposed to be doing on my ranch, Bob?" Jessie asked.

"Now, Jessie, you know I'd never send out anybody to put poison in your tanks," Close protested.

"I'm sorry," Jessie apologized. "I didn't mean that the way it sounded. We've been good neighbors ever since you bought the Cross Spikes, Bob, and I hope we stay that way."

"So do I," Close said. "No offense taken, Jessie. I got a pretty good idea how you're feeling right now."

"You know what I intended to ask you," Jessie went on. "What kind of job was he supposed to be doing when he came on to the Circle Star?"

"I sent him out yesterday to mend fence. My *segundo*

19

told me there was some slack wire and a break or two on the west line, and he was supposed to cover it from the south corner to where my Cross Spikes fence stops at your south fence line, Jessie."

"That was yesterday morning?" Jessie asked.

"It was yesterday noon," Close replied. "I didn't even know that he hadn't come back to the bunkhouse until you and Ki rode up a minute ago."

"What can you tell us about him?" she asked.

"Not much of anything," the Cross Spikes owner replied. "I don't know a single thing about him except his name."

"Did he say where he came from? Or where he was headed?" Ki asked.

"He told me he was just off a job with a ranch in Mexico. He said it was about forty miles west of Nuevo Laredo," Close said, frowning as he prodded his memory. "And I remember him remarking he was going up to the hill country to look for something permanent because he was tired of sweating so much in Mexico."

"That's ranch country, all right," Jessie said. Then, she added, "But I'll bet he didn't tell you the brand he'd been working for."

"Come to think of it, he didn't," Close replied. "He made a pretty good hand, though, the little bit of time he worked here. He knew what to do when it came to wrangling cattle."

"He was riding a horse with your brand on it," Ki said. "I guess he rode in here on his own horse, didn't he?"

"Oh, sure," Close said, "one of those brown Mexican nags that's so dark it looks black. I remember being surprised when I saw he wasn't leading a back-up pony, though, like most saddle tramps traveling a long ways. It struck me as being funny, cheap as horses are down below the border."

"And he'd been here two or three weeks?" Ki asked.

"Something like that," Close said. "I remember thinking

20

yesterday that I had to add him to my payroll next week."

"He hadn't been here long enough to hit a payday, then?" Jessie asked.

Close shook his head. "Close to three weeks, like I just told Ki."

"What was he like, Bob?" Ki asked. "Talkative or quiet? Did he mix with your other hands or act like a loner?"

"I can't tell you all that much about him," Close admitted. "I never had any of the other hands complain to me about him, and my *segundo* never mentioned him, so I suppose he got along with them."

"One thing struck me as being odd," Jessie said. "There weren't any saddlebags on the pony Bannon was riding."

"Well, he wasn't supposed to be out except that one day," Close told her. "He was supposed to be back in time for supper."

"But what I'm getting at is whether there were saddlebags on the horse Bannon was riding when he first got here," she persisted. "When he first asked you for a job, I mean."

"I don't remember seeing any," Close replied, "but let's put it this way, if a saddle tramp stopped here and asked for a job, and he didn't have any saddlebags, I'd've sure noticed because that'd have been a signal something was wrong with him."

"I see what you're getting at," Jessie said. "Would you mind if Ki and I looked through his saddlebags?"

"Well, since Bannon's dead, he won't object," Close said. "And I'll have to look through them myself, so let's go through them together."

Jessie and Ki followed Close to the bunkhouse. The hands hadn't returned from their chores yet, so it was deserted. Close went to one of the bunks, looked under it, and pulled out a pair of scuffed, worn saddlebags. He dumped their contents on the bunk. There'd been very little in them:

a pair of longjohns, a couple of shirts, a pair of jeans, some scattered unmatched socks, a razor, a half-filled box of .45 caliber shells, and an almost full box of ammunition for a .38-.40 Winchester.

"He traveled light," Close commented, "but most saddle tramps do. Go ahead and look at whatever interests you."

"We've already learned something about him just by looking at what was in his saddlebags," Jessie said slowly. "There's not a thing in here that's personal—no letters, no little trinkets, no souvenirs. Any man who doesn't have something that reminds him of the places he's been and the people he's run into generally has something to hide."

"I never thought about that," Close said. "But you're right, Jessie. Most of the hands have some kind of little geegaws or letters or something they set a lot of store by."

Ki had picked up Bannon's jeans and was going through their pockets. He brought out a small square of paper folded and refolded until it was no larger than a postage stamp. Unfolding its creases carefully, Ki looked at it for a moment and then handed it to Jessie.

"Bannon missed one thing when he was cleaning out his gear," he said, "and it might just be the thing we need to put us on his trail."

Jessie looked at the paper. It was not much bigger than her hand. "A hotel bill!" she exclaimed. "From the Cattleman's Rest in San Antonio!" A frown creased her face as she continued to study the slip of paper. Turning to Close, she asked, "Didn't you say just a minute ago that Bannon told you he'd come here from Mexico?"

Close nodded. "And the way he talked, I figured he was telling the truth."

"This hotel bill's made out to J. Bannon," Jessie told Close. "It's for six weeks rent for room thirty-six and it's dated a month ago yesterday."

"That doesn't make sense," Close stated. "Bannon's been here three weeks. Why'd he be paying rent on a hotel room in San Antonio?"

"I can think of one reason," Ki said. "He might've needed a place to leave his gear, and a cheap hotel room is about the best storage he'd be likely to find."

"That's possible, of course," Jessie said thoughtfully.

"I can't argue that," Close said. "So it stands to reason he must've lied to me about just coming up from below the border, but I sure can't say why he'd want to do that."

"There's only one reason I can think of," Jessie replied. "He came to you asking for a job because the Cross Spikes is right next to the Circle Star."

"You mean he was using my place just to get close to yours? Just so he could poison your cattle?" the Cross Spikes owner asked. He shook his head. "Now, that's swinging a pretty big loop, Jessie."

"No," Jessie said firmly. "I don't want to go into details now, Bob. I'll just have to ask you to take my word for what I know is true."

"Well, I sure don't have any reason to doubt you," Close told her. "As long as I've known you, and your daddy before you, I've never had either one of you lie to me."

Jessie nodded her thanks and turned to Ki. "We'd better get back to the Circle Star because as soon as we can get ready to travel, we're heading for San Antonio!"

Chapter 3

Jessie and Ki spent the next two days making preparations, but as Jessie had pointed out, the big ranch was vulnerable to so many kinds of attack that all they could do was to keep the hands alerted. Before leaving, they'd spent more than an hour with Ed Wright, arranging for him to post guards at the most vulnerable tanks and to maintain a patrol on the parts of the range where cattle grazed. In the late evening of the third day, they stepped off the train at the Southern Pacific depot in San Antonio and took a cab to the Menger Hotel.

"I don't know of a hotel here called the Cattleman's Rest," Jessie said while they were riding down Commerce Street from the depot to the hotel. "Do you, Ki?"

Shaking his head, Ki replied, "No, but I'm sure there must be one. It's probably out by the stockyards."

"They'll be able to tell us at the Menger," Jessie said. "And I'm sure you're right. But we'll know before very long."

In the living room of the suite that Jessie maintained permanently at the Menger, she and Ki had a late supper. "We've just put some busy days behind us, Ki," Jessie said as they left the table and settled into easy chairs to drink their coffee. "Let's don't start investigating that Bannon fellow tonight, Ki. This will be the first night in almost a week when we haven't had to sleep with one eye open wondering if the cartel will attack us. Suppose we wait until tomorrow to start looking into this Bannon fellow."

Ki nodded. "It's not going to be easy, Jessie. We don't have much to go on."

"I'm only sure of one thing right now," Jessie went on. "Bannon didn't carry poison and get himself a job on the ranch next to the Circle Star just because he liked to travel."

"You put it very convincingly." Ki smiled. "But I'm as certain as you are that if we can find a crack that Bannon's left and manage to squeeze through it, we'll uncover his cartel connection."

"At least we've got a starting point," Jessie said. "The desk clerk tried to keep from looking surprised when I asked him about the Cattleman's Rest, but I got the impression that it's not a very respectable hotel. And it's where you thought it might be, out by the stockyards. The clerk said we can't miss it if we just go south on Flores Street."

"I had an idea when I first woke up this morning," Jessie told Ki as they sat down to a late breakfast. "And the more I think about it, the better it seems."

"Go on," Ki said when she paused, "I'm listening."

"We've got to make the best use we can of our time here in San Antonio," she went on. "Suppose you check the hotel, and I'll go to see the police and the Texas Rangers and try to find out if Bannon has a record. The more I consider that story he told Bob Close about having been working in Mexico, the more likely it seems that he might've been forced to go down there to hide from the law."

"It wouldn't surprise me," Ki agreed. "And the cartel bosses brought him back here when they decided to make another attack on the Circle Star. They needed somebody who knew about ranching."

Jessie glanced at the ormolu clock ticking on the mantel.

26

She said, "We'll meet back here at noon and compare notes before we decide what to do next."

In the bright morning sunlight, Flores Street had a battered, sleazy look. Ki gazed out of the horse-drawn car. The car had open sides and a bench down its center. A half dozen passengers sat on the bench and four or five more stood on low steps, clinging to metal pipes. Only a few scattered buildings that lined the wide street had started off as dwellings. Most of them had been stores, but now most of these had been turned into residences, for children were playing in their narrow yards and on the margins of the unpaved street. Suddenly, as though some invisible line had been crossed, the buildings came to an end. The gravelly street with the tracks down its center deteriorated into a well-beaten dirt trail.

Ki got a whiff of an alien scent. He looked ahead and saw the stockyards, a broad expanse of planked fences enclosing scores of small corrals. As the car advanced, the breeze grew heavier with the taint of manure picked up from the pens.

Beyond the stockyard fences, the street widened and came to life again in a double row of buildings. As the streetcar moved past the pens, Ki could see the backs and bucking heads of cattle. The car stopped where the rows of buildings began, and the two or three passengers still aboard stepped off, leaving Ki alone on the long seat. His attention was on the buildings ahead.

There were few pedestrians on the street, and most of the buildings were saloons or gambling parlors. Four or five of the larger structures were hotels or boarding houses. The car began moving again, and as it passed the most imposing boarding house, a rambling, deteriorating three-story building, he saw the name CATTLEMAN'S REST HOTEL on the wooden awning that sheltered its entrance. Ki was facing the street on the opposite side of the building and had turned in his seat to look back at it when the car came to a halt.

"All out!" the conductor sang. "End o' the line, mister, unless you figure on riding back to town."

Ki stepped off and stood completing his interrupted scrutiny of the Cattleman's Rest while the conductor unhitched the horse and moved it to the opposite end of the car. He waited until the car moved away on its return trip to town before crossing the street and heading for the hotel.

Though the building was impressively large, it was badly in need of paint and some corrective carpentry. The boards of its awning were split and some of the roof shingles were curling up, while others showed jagged edges where triangles of the loose-grained cedar had dropped out. A few of the windowpanes were cracked, and sheets of newspaper had been pasted over them from the inside. As he mounted the half dozen steps that led to the entrance, the thick planks creaked.

Ki went inside. The place apparently had no lobby, just a small entry hall. A wide shelf barred the way to another door. A call bell stood on the shelf and cubicles for keys took up one of the side walls. At each end of the entry there were doors and steps leading to upper floors.

After Ki had waited for a moment and no one appeared, he tapped the call bell. The tinkle of the bell brought no response. He was reaching to tap it again when the door behind the shelf opened and a burly man, who looked more like a saloon bouncer than a hotel clerk, came into the cubicle behind the desk.

"You looking for a room?" he asked. "If you are, you might as well try at the Eagle House down the street. We don't take Mescins here."

Ignoring the man's surly tone and the racial slur, Ki saw

his best chance to get any information was to play a role. He said, "I am not looking for lodging, *señor*. I have a message to give a man named Bannon."

"Oh." The clerk nodded. "Well, far as I know, Joe ain't got back yet from wherever he went off to, but his old lady's up in the room. At least, I ain't seen her go out yet today."

Ki noted the discrepancy in names and decided to ignore it for the moment. He asked, "It will be all right for me to give the message to her?"

"How in hell do I know? Go ask her yourself," the clerk replied. He gestured toward one of the stairways. "Top floor, room thirty-six."

During the few moments it took Ki to climb the stairs, he tried to concoct a plausible reason for his visit, concluded that he lacked the information required to come up with a convincing story, and decided to play his messenger role by ear. He found the room and tapped lightly. There was no reply, so he tapped a second time.

"Who is it?" a woman's voice called through the door.

"I am looking for Mr. Bannon," Ki replied.

A key grated in the lock and the door opened. The woman who stood in the doorway was either an old thirty or a young forty. She was about Ki's height, but he could not tell whether she was thin or buxom, for the wrinkled wrap she clutched to her throat fell in a straight line from her shoulders and gave no hint as to her figure. Her face showed the beginning of crow's feet at the corners of her dark eyes; the lines that ran from her narrow nostrils to the corners of her full lips could have come from age or a life lived at too fast a pace. Her blond hair was beginning to show dark at its roots.

"Joe's not back yet," she said. "What'd you want with him, anyhow?"

"I have a message for him," Ki told her. "Will he be back soon?"

29

"Your boss ought to know that better than I would," she said. "Joe keeps telling me he's got orders not to talk about where he goes or what he does."

Ki improvised quickly. He said, "The big boss is gone for a week or two. The man he left in charge told me to come find"—he hesitated momentarily, not certain which of Bannon's two first names to use, and then went on—"to find out whether Bannon might have gotten back earlier than he'd planned."

"Well, he hasn't," she replied. "And you can tell your boss I'm just about going crazy from being cooped up in this damn room all by myself."

"You haven't been outside?"

"Now, would I be getting the willies if I could go out, have a drink, and talk to somebody but myself?" she demanded. "And while I'm thinking about it, you better come in and let me close the door. Joe said I wasn't to go out or talk to anybody, but since you and him work for the same boss, I don't guess it'd hurt if I talked to you a few minutes."

"Of course, it wouldn't," Ki replied.

He stepped into the room. The shade at its single window was drawn, softening the light inside. The room was sparsely furnished. A bed stood along the back wall, its covers tangled. On the top of the bureau standing against a side wall, there was a scattering of cosmetics and a half-empty bottle of whiskey. There was a chair beside the end of the bureau, another near the bed. A pile of saddle gear topped by a pair of carpetbags occupied one corner.

"You want a drink?" she asked.

"No, thanks," Ki said, "but you go ahead if you'd like to have one."

"I've already had a couple since I woke up, but I don't guess another little sip would hurt," she observed. Lifting the bottle, she took a healthy swallow, then sat down in the chair at the end of the bureau, and motioned for Ki to take the other. She started to put the bottle back on the bureau, hesitated for a moment, and tilted it to her lips again.

Ki said, "I don't guess you've had a letter from Bannon lately?"

"You know I haven't," she frowned. "Don't you know the boss won't let his men write letters except to him when they're out on a job?"

"I just started in my job a little while ago," Ki replied quickly. "There are a lot of things I don't know about it yet."

"You mind if I ask you something?"

"No," he told her. "Go ahead."

"What kind of Mexican are you? You're a lot lighter than most of 'em I've seen around here."

Ki debated for a second before deciding that from what she'd said the woman knew nothing about the real nature of the work Bannon had been doing and even less about the cartel. He said, "I'm not Mexican, Miss—"

"Didn't they even tell you my name?" she asked.

Ki shook his head and said, "All I knew was that you were in this room at the hotel."

"Well, you can call me Cora. Go on—if you're not Mexican, what are you?"

"Half Japanese, half American."

"Well, I'll be damned! Joe's boss sure does hire a lot of foreigners! The last job Joe went out on he had a German with him, and the one before that there was a Frenchman along. But you haven't told me your name yet."

"Ki."

"Well, us getting acquainted calls for another drink, Ki," Cora said. She tilted the bottle again, put it down, exhaled gustily, and then went on, "You think Joe's boss sending for him means he'll be coming back pretty soon? I'm getting

31

real lonesome here by myself. You're the first company I've had since Joe left."

"I don't know, Cora," Ki said evasively. "All they told me to do was to stop here and see if he was back."

Cora did not reply for a moment; she was staring at Ki's crotch. She realized with a start that Ki was no longer talking and lifted her eyes to his face.

"I can't stand being by myself, all shut up this way," she said tensely. Anger creeping into her voice, she went on, "Joe knows that, damn it! He knows I've got to have a man around!"

Ki saw that Cora was half-drunk. He said, "Well, I wish I could help you, but I don't see—"

"Oh, you can help me, Ki," she broke in. "I haven't been by myself this long for—well, for quite a while." Her eyes dropped to Ki's crotch again as she went on, "I know what I need, if you feel like giving it to me."

"Hold on, Cora," he protested. "What about Joe?"

"Joe won't have to know about it unless you tell him. You wouldn't do that, would you?" Without waiting for Ki to reply, she rushed on, "I damn sure won't. How about it, Ki?"

Before Ki could reply, Cora stood up and stepped quickly to his chair. Dropping to her knees, she began fumbling at his crotch.

"Wait, Cora," Ki said. "I don't think you've thought enough about Joe."

"Damn Joe!" She interrupted him. "He knows how I am when I don't get taken care of regular! But like I said just now, Ki, he never will know."

Cora's hands were on Ki's crotch now, seeking the opening of his fly. She got it open just as Ki reached for her wrists, but she evaded his hands long enough to slip hers into the opened fly and grasp his flaccid shaft. Ki pulled at

32

her wrists, but she resisted by pushing at his forearms with her shoulders. She clutched him stubbornly with her hands so that he knew he'd now run the risk of being hurt if he tried to pull her away.

Facing a situation in which he'd never been caught before, Ki's fatalism ruled his decision. There was still a lot that he needed to learn from her, he reminded himself, and he'd learned from experience that women in the afterglow of satisfaction tend to grow confidential. He stopped struggling, and when Cora felt him relaxing, she freed Ki's shaft from his trousers.

"That's better," Cora sighed, gazing at what she now cradled in her palms. "Just keep still a minute while I get this fellow ready to do the job I've got waiting."

Bending forward, she took him into her mouth and began to flick him with her tongue while rotating her head slowly. Ki had contained himself for a long time, but now that he'd committed himself he saw no reason not to cooperate with her. He let his erection grow, and as it swelled Cora began to purr like some great cat. A soft throaty murmur did not keep her from continuing her avid caresses.

During their brief scuffle, Cora's wrap had fallen loose and in its shadowy folds Ki glimpsed her breasts swaying. He leaned forward as best he could and extended his hands to cradle them for a moment before rubbing them with his thumbs. Cora shuddered as she felt the rasping of Ki's iron-hard thumbs caressing her, and the pressure of her lips and the snakelike movements of her tongue quickly brought him fully erect.

Lifting her head, Cora looked up at him. "I never would've guessed you were so hung," she said. "And I'll bet you're ready to ride me about now."

Ki was fully committed by this time. "Whatever you say," he told her.

33

"Then let's do it, damn it!" she exclaimed.

Rising to her feet, Cora let her loose wrap drop. She stood naked, her full breasts swaying, their tips protruding like pink fingertips. She waited until Ki stood up, her eyes fixed on his jutting shaft as he let his trousers fall to the floor, stepped away from them, and then shrugged out of his jacket. When he moved toward her, Cora leaned forward and grasped the back of the chair, her feet spread wide apart, dark moist curls glistening in the room's dim light.

Looking at Ki from over her shoulder, she said, "Come on, now! Ride me like a stallion, Ki!"

Ki did not wait. He placed his rigid shaft and thrust, a fierce deep penetration that brought a small cry of joy bubbling from Cora's throat. She arched and leaned still further.

"That's it!" she said, her voice trembling in a hoarse whisper. "Now ride me, Ki! Rise me hard and fast!"

Grasping her hips, Ki obeyed. He started stroking, and before he'd gone into her a dozen times with deep swift penetrations, Cora began trembling in ecstatic spasms. Her hips bucked so furiously in response to Ki's thrusts that he had to tighten his grip to keep from losing her.

Cora was crying out now, her words unintelligible, as she rocked under Ki's rhythmic lunges. Her orgasm continued as Ki kept driving until at last her frantic shudders eased. Her cries faded to sighs and he felt her grow limp.

Ki was still far from being finished. He drew away from Cora in spite of her throaty protests, picked her up, and carried her two steps to the bed. After lowering her to the touseled linens, Ki joined her. Though Cora was still whimpering in the aftermath of her spasms, she groped for Ki's swollen shaft, guided him, and then fell back with a prolonged sigh as she felt him thrust into her again.

"Oh, that's good, Ki!" she whispered. "This is just what I need! Go on, don't wait! And keep going as long as you can!"

Ki responded to Cora's frantic plea. He moved slowly for a while, driving in deep, deliberate thrusts until Cora started trembling toward another orgasm. He held still, buried full length, until her quivers faded. Then, he started to stroke again. She was slower to arouse this time, and Ki did not try to hurry her, for he was building to his own spasm. He thrust in a more deliberate rhythm until Cora started shaking gently and moans of pleasure began bubbling from her throat.

Ki was ready now. He held back until Cora burst into a final, convulsive climax and then let himself go. He stiffened and trembled as he jetted and drained, then let himself relax on her soft cradling body.

Cora broke the silence first. She sighed deeply and stirred and Ki lifted himself off her soft body and lay down beside her. After a moment she said, "I feel like you stayed in me for a week, Ki. It still feels good, too."

"I'm glad I pleased you, Cora," Ki said.

"Pleased me, hell!" she replied. "I feel like I'm five pounds lighter and ten years younger!" After a moment of silence, she went on, "Listen, Ki, I don't know whether you've got a wife or not, but—"

"I haven't," Ki interrupted.

"That makes it better," Cora continued. "What I was gong to say is, the rent's paid here till Joe gets back. How'd you like to stay with me till then?"

Ki hadn't expected such an offer. He thought fast, then said, "That could mean a lot of trouble for both of us, Cora."

"You mean if he caught us together?" When Ki nodded, she went on, "You've both got the same boss, Ki. You ought to know when he's coming back, or you could find out."

"I don't know, though," Ki replied. "The only one who knows that is his boss." Feeling that he was making a safe gamble, he asked, "Which one of the bosses does Joe work for?"

35

"You mean there's more than one boss?"

"Didn't you know that?"

"I sure didn't. The only one I know about is Mr. Sloan."

"Frank Sloan? Or—" Ki paused, hoping Cora would answer without thinking.

She did. "No. Al Sloan," she said. "I never heard Joe say anything about Frank."

Thinking quickly, Ki said, "Al is Frank's brother."

"Don't you and Joe have the same boss?" she asked.

"No. I'm not important enough to have just one boss," Ki told her. "Everybody's my boss, Cora. And speaking of bosses, I'd better get back and tell them Joe's not here yet."

Cora rolled over and pinned Ki to the mattress. "One more time," she said, her hand going to his crotch. "I'll get you up again and then I want to straddle you. It might be a long time before Joe gets back, and I've got a feeling you won't be coming to see me anymore."

Chapter 4

Jessie had reached the police station at about the time Ki was arriving at the stockyards. Like all the local government offices in San Antonio, the station occupied one of the ancient adobe buildings on Military Plaza, relics of the original Spanish garrison that had been posted in the city.

"My name is Jessica Starbuck." Jessie introduced herself. The police chief rose from a creaking swivel chair behind his battered desk as she came into his office.

"Miss Starbuck," the chief said curtly, "I'm Mart Lister. What did you want to—" He paused and his eyes widened. "Starbuck? Would you be Alex Starbuck's daughter?" When Jessie nodded, Lister went on, his manner changing from bored indifference to active interest. "I met your daddy a time or two. He was a fine man. I guess you're living on that big spread he was putting together when I met him? Down in the southwest part of the state?"

"Yes," Jessie replied evenly. "The Circle Star."

"Well, now. How can I help you, Miss Starbuck?"

"A number of steers were poisoned down on the Circle Star a few days ago," Jessie explained. "The man who put out the poison was killed while we were trying to capture him, but we've found out that he started for the ranch from San Antonio."

"I guess I don't follow you," Lister said. "You say this man's dead, so what good—"

"Excuse me, Chief Lister," Jessie broke in. "I have a very good reason to believe that someone here in San Antonio sent that man to the Circle Star to spread the poison. Whoever sent him is still alive, and I want to find him."

"I get it, now," Lister said. "You're backtracking this dead fellow, trying to run down his boss."

"Exactly," Jessie said. "I thought the dead man might have a police record here. If so, perhaps there'd be names of his associates in the files you keep."

"Now, that's right shrewd figuring," the police chief said. "He might be in our files. What'd you say this dead crook's name was?"

"I don't think I mentioned it, and I'm not sure the name I have is really his. I'm going by a hotel bill we found in his pocket. The name on it is J. Bannon."

"Bannon," Lister repeated. "J. Bannon." He shook his head thoughtfully. "I don't recall it, but we've got a lot of names in our files. I'd better get my clerk to check for you."

"I'd appreciate it," Jessie nodded.

Lister was gone for a few minutes and when he came back he shook his head before Jessie could ask the question poised on her lips. He said, "This fellow Bannon might be on file somewhere else, Miss Starbuck, but he's not in ours. Is that all you know about him?"

"I could give you his description, but that might fit ten or twenty other criminals, and I don't think it would help."

"Crooks change names faster'n most men change their socks," the chief said. "Now, I don't mean to butt into your business, but you might find out something if you asked about this dead fellow at the hotel he got that receipt from. I guess it was a San Antonio hotel, since you came here to check it."

"Yes. A place called the Cattleman's Rest."

Lister shook his head. "That's not the sort of place I'd

recommend you going to, Miss Starbuck. And it's outside the limits of my authority, so I can't be of much help to you in finding out anything there."

"Don't worry about that, Chief Lister," Jessie said. "I have someone out at the hotel now making inquiries."

"Well, if you come up with anything else—" Lister stopped suddenly. He then went on, "That ranch of yours is a long way outside my jurisdiction, too, Miss Starbuck, but the Texas Rangers might know something about this Bannon."

"I haven't talked to them," Jessie stated.

"Their office is just across the plaza, a little 'dobe building. Talk to Ira Aten. Even if he's not what you'd call an old-timer, I don't suppose there's much of Texas he hasn't covered."

"That's a very good idea, and I thank you for the suggestion. I'll go and talk to him right now."

Angling across the square, Jessie went into the small, squat building that the police chief had described. A saddled horse, ready to ride, stood at a rail to one side of the building and the star emblem of the Texas Rangers adorned the door. A surprisingly young man—he could not have been out of his twenties—rose from the chair at the desk in one corner.

Nodding to Jessie, he asked, "Can I help you, miss?"

"I hope so. You are Ranger Aten, I suppose?"

"Yes, ma'am. Ira Aten's my name, all right."

"Chief Lister suggested that I come talk to you. My name is Jessica Starbuck."

"I recognize your name, Miss Starbuck, even if we haven't met before. You're from the Circle Star Ranch, I imagine," Aten said, as he pulled a chair from the wall and placed it at the corner of his desk.

"Yes. And I'm looking for some information."

"Well, you might as well be comfortable while we talk,

Miss Starbuck. Won't you sit down?" Waiting until Jessie was seated, the ranger settled back in his own chair and asked, "Now, what kind of information are you after?"

"I'm trying to track down the people who hired a man to poison some of my cattle, Mr. Aten."

Aten said thoughtfully, "The way you put that, I get an idea that the man who did the poisoning was caught?"

"Not caught," Jessie corrected him, "killed. We found a room receipt from a hotel here in San Antonio when we searched his belongings. The bill was made out to J. Bannon, and that's all I have to go on. The police didn't have his name in their records, but the chief thought you might've heard of him."

"I know the name Bannon, but I haven't heard it for quite a while. He calls himself either Joe or Jack, and he's a loner, or was when he was alive. A killer, too, I might tell you. He's been on our wanted list for five or six years."

"You can scratch his name off your list," Jessie told the ranger. "I saw him shot."

"You're sure the man was Bannon?"

"Reasonably sure. It isn't often that a man carries around a hotel bill made out to somebody else."

"That's true," the Ranger said. "What hotel was it?"

"A place called the Cattleman's Rest. I've found out it's near the stockyards."

"It's also a place where most of the crooks who know their way around Texas head when they get to San Antonio, Miss Starbuck," Aten said. "I don't suppose you've been there?"

"No. Chief Lister advised me not to. He suggested that I talk to you before going out there."

"That's understandable," Aten stated. "Chief Lister's fairly new in his job, and Cattleman's Rest is just south of the city limits, so it's outside his jurisdiction."

"Yes, the chief mentioned that to me."

"That's why he sent you to me," the ranger went on. "If this Bannon fellow stayed there regularly, I may find out something for you. It'd help if I had that hotel bill you mentioned. Do you happen to have it with you?"

"Of course—right in my purse," Jessie replied. She took out the bill and handed it to the ranger.

Aten glanced at the receipt, then stood up, saying, "I'll ride out there right now and ask a few questions."

Jessie's first thought was of Ki, though she was not really worried about him. Enough time had passed since they left the Menger for Ki to have finished making his inquiries. She was confident that he could handle any situation that developed, but neither of them had anticipated bringing the Texas Rangers into their search or into their fight against the cartel.

As she stood up, she said, "I'm as interested in finding out about Bannon as you are. I suppose that's your horse at the rail outside?"

"Yes," Aten said, "but I—"

Before he could continue, Jessie said quickly, "I'm not asking you to arrange for my transportation, Mr. Aten. I just want to be sure I'll recognize your horse. I'll hire a hack and ride out myself, if you don't mind. I'd like to know as soon as possible what you find."

"I don't guess there's any way to stop you, even if I wanted to, which I don't," Aten told her. "Just like any other citizen in Texas, you're entitled to do whatever you please, as long as you don't get in the way of my business."

"I'll try to stay out from underfoot," Jessie promised. As she started for the door, she said over her shoulder, "I'll look for you at the Cattleman's Rest."

Two or three idle hacks stood in front of the City Hall across the street from the ranger's office. Jessie whistled for one, and within minutes after Aten had ridden off she was following him. She lost sight of the ranger's tall figure in the busy traffic on Commerce Street, and by the time the cab turned into Flores Street, Aten was nowhere to be seen.

After the hack passed the stockyards and entered the cluster of saloons and gambling halls and sleazy hotels, Jessie spotted the Cattleman's Rest at once. Leaning forward, she told the driver to pull up across the street from it, and she leaned forward on the seat, studying the place.

She saw Ira Aten's horse standing at the hitching rail and was just settling back into the seat when a window on the third floor was raised and she saw a man's head and shoulders emerge from it. Even at a distance, Jessie recognized Ki. He was looking along the street, and before she could move to get out of the cab, he levered himself out of the window. Twisting in midair with the skill acquired by endless hours of practice, Ki dropped and caught the windowsill where he clung by his fingers.

Jessie scrambled out of the hack. "Down here, Ki!" she called. Then, as Ki turned his head to look for her, she saw at once that there was no way for her to reach him. Nor was there a way for him to reach her.

Realizing that Ki must have had a compelling reason to leave the hotel by the window, Jessie began looking for a way to help him. Ki was glancing from side to side, studying the sheer bare wall on both sides of him. The hotel had been built with overlapping siding boards, and their sheer drop was broken only by the protruding casings of the two lines of windows that marked the second floor and the third floor where Ki dangled. The row of second-floor windows was a yard or more below Ki's dangling feet.

Suddenly, Jessie saw Ki begin moving, swinging himself from side to side like a pendulum, parallel to the wall. Although she had watched Ki use the *ninjutsu* art to cross

42

vertical surfaces that seemingly had nothing to cling to, Jessie's jaw dropped when at the apex of his sidewise swing Ki released his grip on the windowsill. As he flew through the air, his body slanted to the ground and scraping the building's vertical wall, Jessie saw Ki's objective, the second-floor windowsill. His toes touched it with only an inch or so to spare.

With the impetus of his leap carrying him sidewise, Ki used his toehold on the windowsill to kick upward. He shot up parallel to the wall, arms stretched above his head. His fingers rose above the bottom sill of the next third-floor window and closed on the sill. Without breaking the rhythm of his precarious movements, Ki gained the second window and the third.

Now, only one window remained between Ki's swaying body and the corner of the building. Jessie saw that he would need help and quickly scrambled back into the hack.

"Turn your rig to the left," she commanded the driver. As she spoke, Jessie was digging into her purse. She took out two double eagles and held them in front of the bewildered man's face. "I want you to cross the street and go into the space between the hotel building and that saloon next to it."

"Lady, there ain't room!" he protested. "If I try to pull in there, it's likely to knock a wheel off my—"

"If you wreck this cab, I'll buy you a new one!" she said, moving her hand with the money in it before the man's face. "Now, whip your horse and start moving!"

For a moment the man did not stir, but the two gold pieces Jessie was holding in front of his eyes jolted him into action. He slapped the reins on his horse's back and, as the animal started moving, pulled the left rein. The horse responded faster than its driver. The carriage moved across the street and with only inches to spare on each side went

43

into the narrow space between the hotel and the saloon next to it.

"Pull up!" Jessie ordered, her voice sharp.

Accustomed to obeying his customer's sudden commands, the driver reined in just as Ki's feet landed on top of the vehicle. The thin roof of the cab creaked, but it held.

"Go farther between these buildings," Jessie told the driver.

He slapped the reins. The horse moved ahead, clearing the walls on each side by a few inches, and emerged from the narrow opening at the back of the hotel.

Glancing ahead, Jessie saw no fences. "Just keep right on going," she told him, extending her hand with the coins in it. After the man took them, she went on, "You can cut across those fields after you get past the buildings. Then pull on to the street and go directly to the Menger Hotel when we get back to town."

As the cab moved slowly forward over the rough ground behind the buildings, Jessie heard Ki's sandled feet scuffing on the roof and leaned forward to open the door. Ki swung into the cab and settled down on the seat beside Jessie.

"I'm glad you saw what I was planning to do," he told Jessie. "There wasn't any way to tell you that I could not see enough holds to make my *ninjutsu* moves possible. That ranger had already knocked twice, and he was threatening to kick the door open, so I had to get out fast."

"I'm sorry you got an unpleasant surprise, Ki," Jessie replied. "The ranger suddenly made up his mind to go check the hotel, and there wasn't any way I could stop him or get there ahead of him and warn you. All I could do was hope that you'd finished searching Bannon's room and left before he got there."

"It wasn't just Bannon's room," Ki said. "He left a woman in it."

"Alive, I hope?" Jessie asked.

"Oh, yes. The only problem was that she didn't have any idea where Bannon had gone, what he was supposed to do, or when to expect him back."

"Or who hired him either, I suppose?"

"All that she knew was a name, Sloan. I did manage to get a first name out of her. Sloan's first name is Al—Albert, I suppose."

"And you didn't have time to search the place because you'd spent so much time questioning her," Jessie said.

"I was just beginning to search it," Ki said. "He left some gear there, but it was all in a pile. I hadn't really started looking through it before that ranger knocked."

"So we do have a little more to go on than we had," Jessie said. "And I can go back to the ranger's office and talk to him, so we'll know whether he learned anything useful."

"Oh, we haven't wasted the morning, Jessie," Ki said. "We've got an opening we can slip a lever into—providing we can find a lever."

"Or make one," Jessie said thoughtfully. "Yes, except for one thing, we're better off than when we started, Ki. That woman who was in Bannon's room might tell Ira Aten about you, and if she does, he'll be looking for you."

"Yes." Ki nodded. "She's inclined to talk. And before I thought about what I was doing, I was foolish enough to tell her my name."

"I've already told the cabman to take us to the Menger," Jessie said. "I'll give the ranger time to get back to the office and then go see whether or not you're on his Wanted list. In the meantime, you'd better stay in the hotel."

Jessie and Ki got out at the Menger and were crossing the marble floor of the lobby when one of the bellboys left the bench where he'd been sitting with his fellows and

45

hurried to intercept them before they reached the staircase.

"Excuse me, Miss Starbuck," he said. "There's a gentleman in the dining room who asked me to call him when you came in. Is it all right with you if I tell him now?"

"Did the gentleman give you a name?" Jessie asked.

"Oh, yes, ma'am," the bellhop replied. "He's Mr. Steven Carter."

"I don't suppose he told you why he wants to see me?"

"No, ma'am. But he did say it was important. And he's been waiting almost two hours for you to get back."

Jessie looked at Ki who shrugged to signify that the name was strange to him, too. She told the bellhop, "If he's waited for me that long, it must be important. You can go tell him I'm here."

After the bellhop started across the lobby, Jessie said to Ki, "Whoever this man Carter is, he must've gone to some trouble to find us. Ed Wright is the only one who knows where we are, which means he stopped at the Circle Star."

Both Jessie and Ki were watching the dining room door when the bellhop emerged, followed by a well-dressed man in his middle thirties. He made a beeline to where they were standing.

"Miss Starbuck," he said to Jessie, extending his hand. "My name is Steven Carter, and I'm glad to see you at last."

"You've been looking for me quite a while, then?" Jessie asked as she took the extended hand and shook it.

"Not really very long. I was on my way to your ranch, but when I stopped here between trains and happened to see your name when I signed the register, it seemed too good an opportunity to miss, so I waited."

"Would you like to tell me why you're so anxious to see me, Mr. Carter?" Jessie asked.

"I'd like nothing better. You happen to own a railroad line that my associates and I want to buy."

Chapter 5

"I'm afraid you're mistaken," Jessie said. "The Starbuck interests do include quite a bit of railroad stock, but certainly not enough to control an entire railroad."

"I'm not talking about railroad stock, Miss Starbuck," Carter said. "I don't even know whether the one I'm interested in ever put out stock. All I'm sure of is that it's your property."

"That's utterly impossible!" Jessie exclaimed. "I'm sure I'd know about it if I owned a railroad!"

"Perhaps you'll remember when I've explained the details," Carter went on. "But a hotel lobby's no place for us to talk. I imagine you're ready for lunch, and I was waiting for mine to be served. Why don't you join me in the dining room? We can talk about my offer there."

Jessie had been covertly studying Carter while he talked. Though he was dressed like a city merchant, he looked more like a man accustomed to working outdoors. Carter was taller than Ki. His complexion was the tan that fair outdoorsmen often had. His lips were full, though not too full; he was clean shaven except for full sideburns that in accordance with the current fashion extended halfway to his jawline.

He carried himself erect, his shoulders were broad, his chest deep, and his stomach flat. He was wearing a three-piece business suit and its fit had the unmistakable signs of custom tailoring of a superior quality fabric. His high starched collar and white shirt were crisp—as though they'd been laundered and carefully ironed only minutes ago—and his shoes were neither too pointy nor too broad.

"I've certainly no objection to eating lunch with you, Mr. Carter," Jessie replied. "But I still can't understand where you got the mistaken idea that I have a railroad for sale."

"I'm sure I can explain the misunderstanding, Miss Starbuck," Carter said and smiled. "Shall we go into the dining room?"

"I assume you're including Ki in your invitation?" Jessie asked quickly.

Carter's face showed that Jessie's remark had startled him. He glanced at Ki and said, "Of course, if that's your pleasure." He extended his hand to Ki. "I'm sorry, perhaps I should have introduced myself earlier."

"I have taken no offense, Mr. Carter," Ki said as they shook hands. "But I must join Jessie in telling you that during the years I was with her father, I don't recall that a railroad was ever included in his properties."

"Ki was my father's—" Jessie paused, wrinkled her nose, then went on, "I don't like trite phrases, but he was Alex's righthand man, just as he is mine."

"So I have both of you to convince," Carter remarked as they walked toward the doors to the dining room. "But I'm sure you'll both admit you're mistaken when you hear my explanation."

"I'm eager to hear it," Jessie said as Carter led them to a table set for one, the only food on it a half-emptied bowl of soup.

Seeing them sit down, a pair of waiters hurried to clear the table and add extra plates and utensils. While this was going on and while Jessie and Ki were placing their orders, conversation was impossible. When they'd settled down and Jessie and Ki had ordered, Carter picked up the interrupted conversation.

"Perhaps you were a bit too young to be interested in your father's business affairs when he was developing silver mines in the southwest, Miss Starbuck," he began. "And I doubt that any records of his purchases and sales of silver claims were kept."

Jessie glanced at Ki, her eyes questioning him silently.

"I think Mr. Carter has touched the crux of the matter," Ki said quietly. "While you were still in school in the east, Jessie, Alex disposed of a great deal of property that he said was taking up more time than it was worth. He sold all his silver interests, and since all the operating records went to the buyers, I'm sure nothing except perhaps some sale contracts are left. They'd be in dead storage files that you've never had any reason to look at."

"Ki, are you telling me that Alex might actually have had a railroad at one time?" Jessie frowned.

"I am beginning to remember something, Jessie," Ki said, "but let Mr. Carter go on. I would like to hear his story."

Carter acknowledged Ki's remark with a nod and said, "At the time I'm talking about, most of the prospecting in the Arizona Territory had been done in the central section. But your father was a venturesome man, Miss Starbuck. He reasoned quite correctly that there were fresh opportunities in the southern part."

"Alex was always ahead of his time," Jessie said. "He had a very rare ability to anticipate the future."

"That ability must have been what led him to southern Arizona," Carter went on. "Until your father went down there, nobody had paid much attention to it."

"But Alex was never a prospector," Jessie protested.

"Of course not," Carter agreed. "From what I've learned, he was a financier—a grubstaker, the prospectors called it. He was there long before others, and the men Mr. Starbuck backed did find a number of small silver lodes."

"I think I see what you're getting at," Jessie said. "Alex began developing the lodes the men he'd financed had found."

"Exactly." Carter nodded. "And that brings us to the railroad. I'm sure you've seen that part of the Arizona Territory, Miss Starbuck—"

When Carter paused expectantly, Jessie nodded. "I've seen it. I know it's very rough country, more desert than anything else."

"And as with much industrial processing, water's needed in order to process silver ore," Carter went on. "But Mr. Starbuck got the idea of building a railroad to carry the ore to water instead of trying to find water close to the ore. And that's where the railroad came in. It was built and operated for a few months; then several of the silver claims petered out. A short time later, Mr. Starbuck sold all his silver holdings to a syndicate operating out of Chicago."

Jessie was silent for a moment and then she said, "I'm amazed that you seem to know more about some aspects of my business affairs than I do, Mr. Carter."

"I haven't offended you, have I?" Carter frowned. "I assure you that the only investigation I've made into your father's operations has been in connection with the railroad I'm interested in."

"Oh, I'm not at all upset," Jessie said and smiled. "I've looked into businesses belonging to others myself—when I was interested in buying them. But if Alex had built a railroad, he'd certainly have sold it to the syndicate that bought his mines."

"There's no record that he did," Carter replied. "But no one seems to know exactly what happened because the syndicate that bought the silver mines collapsed and somehow in the bankruptcy proceedings the railroad right of way, the rails, and some water rights were overlooked. The title to them is still in Mr. Starbuck's name, which means that you own them now."

Ki spoke when Carter paused. "I see how that could have happened, now that you've refreshed my memory, Mr. Carter. The sale was quite hurried and all the details were handled in San Francisco. It would have been very easy to have missed including the railroad. As I remember, Alex incorporated it separately from the mines and their machinery and other property."

When Jessie said nothing, Carter picked up the conversation where he'd left off. "I've looked into the condition of the railroad pretty thoroughly, Miss Starbuck. It has about thirty miles of graded right of way in addition to sixty miles of track. If there's any rolling stock, I can't find a record of it. There's going to be a lot of work involved in getting it into operation, but that's not your problem. The only question I need an answer to right now is, are you interested in selling?"

"It's a little hard for me to agree to sell something I didn't even know I owned," Jessie replied. "And Alex taught me never to sell anything until I'd inspected it myself and made my own estimate of its value."

"Does that mean yes or no?" Carter pressed.

"Neither one, Mr. Carter," Jessie replied calmly. "Before I can give you an answer, I'd like to know why you're so anxious to buy an abandoned, decrepit railroad."

"That's very simple. My associates and I have just bought a recently discovered copper lode only a few miles away from some of the silver mines your father sold. We're sure that if we can buy your railroad at a fair price it would be much less expensive to rebuild it on its present right of way

51

than to build one of our own to haul our ore to a smelter."

"I can understand that," Jessie said. "And I suppose you plan to start operating the mines at once?"

"Of course," Carter answered. His voice very serious, he went on, "We're not speculators, Miss Starbuck. We're not selling stock in our venture to the public, if that's what you're thinking."

"It did cross my mind," Jessie said, "but I'm not going to give you an answer until I go and look at what you're asking me to sell."

"A trip to Arizona will take time," Carter said and frowned. "And time is very important to us right now."

Looking across the table at Ki, Jessie asked, "How long do you think it's going to take to finish our business here in San Antonio?"

"It'll depend on what you find out this afternoon," he said.

"Then, I'll tell you this evening when Ki and I can leave for Arizona, Mr. Carter," Jessie said. "But to make waiting easier for you, I will say that at the moment I'm very much inclined to accept a fair offer for the railroad."

"I never thought I'd look forward to getting to a place named Tombstone," Jessie said to Ki, as she turned away from the barren vista that surrounded them. "Right now, I envy Mr. Carter. He'll be quite comfortable on the train going to Tucson."

"I've ridden in more comfortable accommodations," Ki said after he dropped back into place following an especially hard bounce. "But we were smart to leave San Antonio— even though when you visited Ranger Aten you found out that Cora told him nothing and he hadn't seen me leaving Cattleman's Rest."

"Well, Steven Carter's offer came along at the right time,"

Jessie responded. "We had exhausted what San Antonio had to offer about Bannon. Once we conclude our railroad business with Carter, perhaps we can return to pick up the investigation—this time with Ira Aten's valuable help."

When the Southern Pacific train on which they'd traveled from Texas reached Bisbee, a telegram from his associates in the syndicate had been waiting for Carter, and after reading it he turned to Jessie with a concerned frown.

"I'm afraid this is going to interfere with our plans, Miss Starbuck," he said. "My associates in the syndicate are meeting tomorrow in Tucson, and I absolutely must be there."

"Your meeting won't last more than a day or two, will it?" Jessie asked.

"Oh, no. Probably only one day."

"Then, to save time for both of us, suppose Ki and I go on to Tombstone, since you said it's the best place to stay while I'm looking over the road," Jessie suggested. "In this deserted part of the Arizona Territory, you can catch up with us quite easily just by following the old right of way."

"I certainly won't have any trouble doing that," Carter agreed. "Suppose you take the map I made of it. You should be able to cover about half the right of way in a day. Then, you can wait in Tombstone until I get there, and we'll ride the rest of it together."

"A very good idea," Jessie said. "It'll certainly save time for both of us."

Since getting off the train at Bisbee two hours earlier, they'd been bouncing around on the hard seats of a wagon that had been converted into a sort of open carryall by nailing planks across its bed. The uphill road was two lines of ruts, and its twists grew more sinuous than those of a wounded snake as it zigzagged up the sunbaked slopes heading toward Tombstone.

"If I'd known how rough the country is around here, I'd

have brought Sun and a horse for you," Jessie went on, grabbing for the seat to keep from falling out as one side of the wagon lurched when the wheels left the ruts and the seats tilted sharply while on a hairpin curve.

"We can rent horses at a livery stable in Tombstone," Ki said. "Or perhaps we'd better get mules."

"I'll take my chances with a livery horse rather than ride a mule, Ki," Jessie replied quickly, "even though I know I won't find another horse equal to Sun. But let's wait and see what the country's like when we get closer to Tombstone."

Getting closer to Tombstone turned out to be another five hours of jouncing and bouncing through barren country on a road that grew progressively steeper and rougher and more winding the longer they traveled. The sun was hanging low by the time the wagon pulled up over the rim of a broad plateau and they saw a sprawling cluster of buildings only another mile or two ahead.

"I think we've finally arrived, Ki," Jessie said, "and I can't remember when I've been so glad to end a trip before."

Ki was looking at the vista ahead: the town clustered near the center of the plateau, the barren land stretching on all sides to the false horizon of the plateau's end, the real horizon provided by the jagged peaks of mountains in the distance.

Tombstone itself spread with no apparent form or cohesion across a depression in the lumpy surface of the plateau. A pair of small smelters dominated the area directly in front of them, their black tin buildings and tall smokestacks blotting out much of the town itself. As they watched, a ten-mule team hauling a pair of wagons cut across the plateau in front of them and bumped over the hump of ground that led to the smelter.

Brown and tan dominated the landscape. The only vegetation on the ocher earth between the wagon and the town was an occasional clump of pale green yucca. They could see about half the buildings in Tombstone now, and most of these were built of adobe. In the town's center, a handful of buildings rose above the rooflines of the smaller structures, and their painted walls were green and blue and charcoal.

"Tombstone's grown since I was here last," Ki commented as he turned to Jessie after studying the town and its surroundings. "It was just a little clump of houses around a smelter when I visited it with your father, but that was quite a while ago."

"It looks good to me," Jessie said. "But I'm ready to welcome anyplace that will get us out of this wagon. At least it seems big enough to have a hotel or two and maybe even a good restaurant. But we're not going to be here long. Mr. Carter should join us day after tomorrow, and we'll be leaving to look at the railroad."

As the carryall drew closer and they could make out more details of Tombstone's buildings, they began to feel better about their prospects.

As they passed the sign identifying Toughnut Street, the business district started abruptly with a long row of offices on one side, a livery stable and a few residences on the other. Ahead there were stores and saloons lining both sides of the street, and when the rig turned into Allen Street, they could see substantial business buildings on both sides for several blocks.

Along Allen Street signs on the buildings identified the one on the corner as the Pima County Bank, and beyond it there were two saloons, a dry goods store, a saddle shop, a furniture store, and a jewelry store. On the north side of the street there stood two more saloons, another saddle shop, and a small building beside wide gates read OFFICE—OK

CORRAL. The driver reined his team through the gates and pulled the carryall to a stop.

"Let's just wait until the wagon's empty, Ki," Jessie suggested. "It'll be easier to get out our luggage then."

"This is as far as I haul, miss," the wagoneer said when he saw Jessie and Ki still seated. "If you're sitting there trying to figure out where that shooting between the Earp boys and the Clantons took place, it was by that back gate over yonder, and I can tell you just how it all happened. Now,—"

Jessie interrupted him. "I'm not the least interested in hearing about a gunfight. I'm sitting here because—"

This time it was the wagoneer who interrupted. "If you're afraid to get down because you've heard Tombstone's a rough town, you don't have to worry. We've gotten rid of all them Earps, and the Clantons ain't feuding with nobody else. You can walk down any street in town, day or night—"

Jessie broke in for the second time. "We're just waiting until it's less crowded to get our baggage out. As soon as we do, we'll go find a hotel. And that's one way you can help us. Which of the hotels in Tombstone would you say is both clean and quiet?"

"Well, Chris Bilicke's Cosmopolitan Hotel is just a ways back, at the corner where I turned," the man said.

Jessie nodded her thanks and turned to Ki. "I suppose one of the hotels here is as good as another, Ki. And this one seems to be the closest."

"I'll carry the bags," Ki replied.

They walked down Allen Street, passing a restaurant and a small narrow shop selling patent medicines, then went by two more saloons as they headed toward the corner. Before they reached the intersection, Jessie paused and Ki stopped with her.

"Wait a minute, Ki," she said. "I see the hotel sign just across the street, so why don't we have supper now? We're right here in front of a café, and Oriental food will be a welcome change from the steaks and roasts we've been eating lately."

Ki looked at the sign and smiled. It read *Quong Ki's Cancan Restaurant*. He smiled and shook his head. "Even though the proprietor and I share a common name, I think I'd rather have just a quick American-style meal tonight, Jessie. The kind of Oriental dinner you're thinking of would take two hours, and I plan to be in bed before too long."

"Your idea's better than mine, Ki," Jessie said. She pointed up Fourth Street. "How about the Fourth Street Coffee Shop? We should be able to get a simple supper there."

"Yes, it looks all right," Ki said. "Later, I'll get acquainted with Mr. Quong. Since we're both Orientals, he might pass on some information to me that would keep us out of trouble while we're here."

"Now, you know we're not going to have any trouble here, Ki," Jessie replied. "All that we're going to do is take a horseback ride along that old right of way, and if we find what I suspect we will, I'll close a deal with Mr. Carter's syndicate and we'll take the next train back to the Circle Star."

"I'm sure you're right," Ki agreed. "And after all the moving around we've done these last couple of weeks, a rest will be good for both of us."

Chapter 6

"It's a good thing Alex built this railroad in such dry country, Ki," Jessie commented as she and Ki reined in their horses at the bottom of a steep grade and looked up at a gap in the roadbed. "That's the worst gap we've seen so far. I'd hate to have been on a train that hit it."

Four or five of the ties still clung to the twin lines of steel to which they were attached, silhouetted in black against the bright midafternoon sky.

"If they'd been used, the tracks would be in better condition, of course," Ki said. "But since Mr. Carter has told us he's inspected the right of way, I'm sure he knows what's going to be involved in putting it back into usable condition."

"I'm sure he has. But judging by what we've seen so far, I can't honestly ask much for what they're buying," Jessie told him. "I'm inclined to let the syndicate make an offer and accept it without much dickering. Whatever it brings will be found money anyhow."

Jessie and Ki were nearing the end of their second day of inspecting the abandoned railroad. Along the way they'd seen many signs of the prospectors who'd scouted the hillsides ten and twenty years earlier, flocking like sheep when word of a rich strike reached them. The desert country was good at preserving traces of those who had passed through it.

They'd found many small scatterings of black coals where campfires had been kindled, an occasional battered pot or pan discarded, even tattered clothing and worn boots survived in the dry air. They had also come across three or four long mounds of earth, the graves of prospectors who did not survive the desert.

As they toed their horses into motion and rode slowly along beside the decrepit roadbed, Jessie said, "I'll be glad to get back to tombstone tonight. All I can think of right now is soaking for an hour in that bathtub in the hotel and then going to a nice restaurant for a dinner that's a bit more than jerky and cheese and soda crackers."

"How far are we from Tombstone?" Ki asked.

"Not far." Jessie took out the map Carter had given her and unfolded it. Tracing the lines with a forefinger, she went on, "We just follow the rails for another four or five miles to an abandoned mine, then angle west another three miles or so to town."

"We'd better move on, then," Ki suggested, "or we'll be making the last mile or so in the dark."

The sun had dropped almost to the ragged rim of the horizon and the first pink tinge of sunset was coloring the western sky. As their tired horses plodded along, Jessie said to Ki, "I suppose it's the result of the scant meals we've had for the two days we've been out, but I can't seem to get food off my mind. Why don't we try Quong Ki's menu tonight, Ki?"

"A good idea," Ki said. "It'll take him two hours to prepare a really good meal, so when we pass his place on the way to the hotel, I'll stop in and order. Then, our dinner will be ready by the time you've finished soaking and I've had a quick bath."

"We'd better enjoy a good meal tonight," Jessie went on.

"Steve Carter should be here by tomorrow to join us in following the right of way into Bisbee."

"Another two days on the desert, then," Ki said thoughtfully. "Yes, we deserve a good dinner tonight, Jessie. While we're riding the rest of the way into town, I'll be thinking of a menu that will challenge Quong Ki's skill."

Another few minutes brought them to scattered buildings that marked Tombstone's northern outskirts, a few large residences standing in the midst of the foundations for other buildings and homes. Taking a shortcut by zigzagging through the building sites, they emerged on Fremont Street and in the fading light reined the horses into the back gate of the OK Corral.

Ki put both his and Jessie's saddlebags over his shoulders and they walked through the corral and between the stables to emerge at its main entrance on Allen Street. It was the supper hour, and the streets were almost deserted. There were no carriages on the street, and on the board sidewalks they saw only a few miners hurrying home to eat or to one of the score of saloons for a drink.

As they reached the corner, Ki said, "Why don't you just go on to the hotel, Jessie? I'll stop here at the restaurant and order our supper."

"Right now, I'd rather get in a tub of hot water than sit and wait while you order, Ki," she said. "Hand me my saddlebags, and I'll take you up on your suggestion."

Ki watched Jessie while she crossed the street and then went into Quong Ki's restaurant. It was not quite what he'd expected. Aside from a large bronze Buddha on a plinth in one corner, the usual wall decorations of fans and streamers were absent. The tables were filled, and through an archway leading into a second dining room, he got a glimpse of other tables, also occupied. A waiter serving one of the tables near the door looked up and saw Ki. He hastily distributed

61

the three or four bowls still on his tray and hurried to Ki.

Speaking in a Mandarin dialect, he said, "You cannot come in through this door. Go back to the street and enter by the kitchen."

"I did not come here to eat," Ki replied. "I want to order a meal for two to be served later."

"That makes no difference," the waiter said firmly. "You cannot come in through this door."

"Quong Ki does not welcome customers of his own kind?"

"He welcomes them if they follow the rules he sets."

"Only Americans may come in the main door?"

"You have at last understood, I see," the waiter said. "Now, go to the back door and you will be admitted."

Instead of leaving, Ki shifted his position. He put one foot on the sidewalk, the other inside the door, and pressed the center of his back firmly against the door casing.

"What are you doing?" the water asked, frowning.

When he replied, Ki spoke in English. "I am only following Quong Ki's rules. I am half-American. I put that half inside. The Oriental half I leave outside."

"Enough of such foolishness!" the waiter snapped angrily.

He reached for Ki's arm to push him outside the door. Ki grasped the man's extended hand in the simplest of all holds. His fingertips, as hard as iron, dug into the sensitive nerve center at the base of the man's thumb, paralyzing his hand, while with his free hand Ki grabbed the man's fingers and pressed them backward, using his own thumb as a lever while his stiffened fingers served as its fulcrum.

Pain twisted the waiter's face. He threw back his free arm in the beginning of a blow aimed at Ki. Ki applied a bit more pressure and used his hold to swing the man around into a position where he could not land his fist.

Through clenched teeth the waiter gasped, "Let me go,

you tramp! When Quong Ki hears of this he will..." His words trailed off into a moan as Ki put a bit more pressure on.

Without raising his voice, Ki said calmly, "If you do not want your hand to be crippled, you will go and ask Quong Ki to give me the honor of speaking with him."

"Very well," the waiter agreed. "I will do as you ask."

Ki released the man's arm, and with a scowl the waiter started toward the back of the restaurant.

Little more than a minute passed before the waiter returned with a short, chubby-faced Chinese man who wore the thin drooping mustache affected by the elders of his race. Though Ki could not judge his age, the careful manner in which the newcomer moved and the network of tiny wrinkles on his face marked him as well along in years. His lips were compressed angrily, and his eyelids closed slits. He had on much the same kind of clothing Ki was wearing, trousers cut so full that they looked baggy and a loose blouse belted at the waist.

Keeping his voice low and speaking in the same dialect used by Ki and the waiter, he said, "I am Quong Ki. Now, who are you to cause a disturbance in my restaurant?"

"My name is also Ki. And I did not come here to cause trouble, but neither did I come here to be insulted."

"You call it an insult that I ask you to use another door?" Quong Ki asked. "You, who have only half a name?"

"I choose to use only the family name of my mother," Ki replied evenly. "But that is not important. I came here to ask that a special dinner be prepared for the lady it is my privilege to serve."

"And her name is?" Quong Ki asked.

"Her name is Jessica Starbuck."

Quong Ki's manner changed instantly. "Ah!" he exclaimed. "I know now why you were angered! But if you had done as Ah Jin asked, there would have been no need for anger between us. Now, do me the honor of coming with me, Ki. I have something important that I must talk with you about."

Mystified by the sudden change in Quong Ki's manner, Ki followed him through the two dining rooms into the restaurant's bustling kitchen. He was surprised again when the restaurant owner did not stop. He merely caught the attention of one of the half dozen cooks hovering over a line of woks and made a few quick gestures with his fingers, and then he led Ki to a door on the far side of the room.

In contrast to the sparsely decorated dining rooms and kitchen, the room they entered was richly decorated. Two walls were covered with brilliantly lacquered screens, another was hung with delicate gold and silver embroidered silk, and the fourth was broken by small niches holding elaborately carved vases and ivory figurines. Three or four lacquered tables with matching chairs were the only furniture in the room.

Quong Ki motioned for Ki to sit down, and before they could settle into chairs, one of the waiters brought in a tray holding a teapot, two small cups, and a plate of *lichee*. He placed the tray on a table and left as quickly and silently as he had entered.

Quong Ki said nothing until he had poured a small amount of tea into one of the cups, tasted it, and then filled a cup for Ki before filling the one he'd used for tasting.

Ki had been careful to show no surprise at any time during their passage from the restaurant door to the back room. He kept his face impassive now when the restaurant owner spoke to him, changing from Mandarin to Cantonese. Ki understood a bit of the other major Chinese dialect, but was not as schooled in it as he was in Mandarin.

"If you don't object, I prefer that we continue to speak

in Mandarin," he told Quong Ki, "unless you would like to use English."

"I will be glad to," Quong Ki replied in almost unaccented English. "Then, we will be using a language foreign to both of us, and neither will have an advantage."

"You are a surprising man, Quong Ki," Ki said. "And the thing that surprises me most is the change you showed when I mentioned Jessica Starbuck."

"I have good reason. Many years ago in Shanghai, I met her father and was proud to become his friend. He eased me over many bad times. And I knew who you must be when I heard you say his daughter's name."

"We have a common bond," Ki said.

Quong Ki's revelations did not surprise him. He had learned that the Chinese in the United States had kept their family ties alive and that news of interest to them traveled swiftly across the continent. He did not bother to explain his own relationship with Jessie; the restaurant owner's recognition was proof that Quong Ki knew of his connection with her and her father.

Ki paused to sip his tea and then went on, "You must have many sources of information, Quong Ki. Hadn't you heard that Jessie and I arrived in Tombstone two days ago?"

Quong Ki shook his head. "I knew only that a woman with an Oriental man as her companion had taken rooms at the Cosmopolitan Hotel and stayed a night."

"We left the morning after we got here, but only to go and look at an old railroad that Alex built years ago, before Tombstone existed," Ki explained. "Jessie has an offer from some men who want to buy the road."

"Then, you will be here for several days?"

"A day or two, at least," Ki replied. "Jessie is waiting for the man representing the buyers. He should get here from Tucson tonight or early tomorrow."

"But you will bring Miss Starbuck here to meet me?"

"We are planning to have dinner here," Ki replied. "That is why I tried to come in your restaurant a few minutes ago."

"Let me explain why you were refused," the old man said quickly. "Most of the Orientals who have come to Tombstone are Chinese of the coolie class. The miners and storekeepers have small patience with them. If I opened my dining room to the coolies, I would soon lose my trade. But I keep this room we are in for my friends and for Orientals who are strangers and who would not be welcome at other restaurants."

"Since I will be with Jessie, will we eat in here tonight?"

"Of course."

"We'll be here in about an hour then. Jessie and I need to clean up after our two days of traveling. If you'll call one of your waiters, I'll give him our order."

"Allow me to arrange your dinner," Quong Ki said. "I promise you will not be disappointed."

Ki knew what Oriental courtesy demanded. He asked, "Will you do us the honor of dining with us, Quong Ki?"

"I would be very pleased to, Ki. And after dinner, there are things I must ask Miss Starbuck, if you do not think she will object."

"I'm sure she won't," Ki replied. He stood up and bowed. "Until later, Quong Ki."

"I don't know when I've enjoyed such a fine dinner, Quong Ki," Jessie sighed as she put down her teacup. "It was more than just a dinner; it was a banquet."

"It certainly was," Ki seconded. "I'm glad I let you plan it. I wouldn't have thought of ordering some of the dishes in an isolated place like Tombstone. I don't see how you managed to get all the ingredients."

"We have our own resources," Quong Ki said quietly.

"We do not give up our own foods just because we are in America."

"Yes, I can understand that," Jessie said. "Ki said you had some questions to ask me."

"I do, Miss Starbuck," the old Chinese said. He stopped for a moment, frowning, then went on, "You must understand that I do not want to ask about your personal matters. But this concerns you as well as it does my people here in Tombstone."

Even though she did not see where Quong Ki's words were leading, Jessie nodded. "Your questions won't offend me. Go on and ask them."

"Very well," Quong Ki continued. "In my tong I am one of the council of elders. That is why the council asked me to leave my eldest son in charge of my restaurant in Prescott and come here to look after the welfare of our people. And a matter has come up that is beyond my experience, Miss Starbuck. That is why I seek your advice."

"Something that concerns me?" Jessie's voice showed that she was puzzled. "I can't imagine what it could be."

"It concerns a—I can only call it a tong that is not Oriental—that has certain plans regarding Tombstone," the restaurant owner went on.

Ki's instincts sent him a sudden warning signal, but he did not want to interrupt the old man.

"There are many people of my tong here," Quong Ki said. "We have many families in the Arizona Territory because there is work. Now, this new tong has offered us a chance to earn much more if we join forces with them. But I have made inquiries and some of the things I have learned make me uneasy. One of them concerns your father."

"Alex has been dead for a number of years," Jessie said, controlling her voice with great willpower. "How could this, this tong you mention, possibly concern him?"

"To impress us with their power, to tempt us to join them,

67

these men of the new tong have boasted that they have the power of life and death over anyone who opposes them," Quong Ki went on. "And though they did not say this to me, the elder on our council to whom they did say it reported to me that to prove their point they claim to have caused the death of your father."

Chapter 7

For a moment neither Jessie nor Ki spoke. Then, Jessie asked calmly, "How long ago did you hear of this remark, Quong Ki?"

"It has been two weeks now."

"Is the elder who repeated it to you still in Tombstone?" she went on. "May I talk to him?"

Quong Ki shook his head. "Unfortunately, he has gone back to Prescott. You understand, he is a very old man, as I am myself. Old bones do not take kindly to traveling."

Ki asked, "Can you tell me what you and your friend decided to do about this invitation you've received, Quong Ki? Or would it be against your custom to discuss such things with outsiders such as Jessie and me?"

"What we elders talk of is not to be shared, Ki," Quong Ki replied. "But it will do no harm to tell you that we do not decide quickly to do a thing. We are even slower to decide about a thing such as this, for we have never before joined forces with any group except a tong of our own people."

Ki looked questioningly at Jessie, who returned a quick nod to indicate she'd understood the old man's answer to mean that the tong was not likely to make a quick decision.

"Then, find out more about these people before you decide," Jessie urged. "No matter what they tell you, they aren't a tong such as yours. Believe me, Quong Ki, I know about these men. They're outlaws and they don't band together to help people, but to steal from them."

"Is this thing they boast of true, Miss Starbuck?" Quong Ki asked. "Did they cause the death of your father?"

Jessie nodded soberly. "Yes—even if no one can prove it."

Ki saw that Jessie was reluctant to explain. He put in quickly, "They asked Alex Starbuck to join them, Quong Ki. He was as reluctant as you seem to be, so to persuade him they told him what they planned to do. Alex refused to join them and started fighting to keep them from carrying out their plans to get control of America's wealth. That was when they sent a band of killers to cut him down in cold blood. Jessie is too modest to tell you that she is fighting them now, just as her father did."

Quong Ki nodded thoughtfully when Ki had finished. Then, he turned to Jessie and asked, "Is that why you have come here to Tombstone?"

"No," she said. "As Ki told you, I came here on business. Neither of us had any idea that we'd run into something such as you've just told us."

"Then, you will not be here long?" he asked.

Jessie shook her head. "A day or two longer."

"And Ki will go with you?"

"Of course. Why do you ask, Quong Ki?"

"I have been thinking," he said slowly. "There are no other elders of my tong close enough to Tombstone to get here quickly if I should need help in handling its affairs."

"You must make all the decisions alone?" Ki asked.

"If I need to consult quickly with one of the other elders, there is a Western Union office in the jewelry store just up the street. But I do not like to have my words read by any other than the elder for whom they are intended."

Ki nodded. "I can understand that, Quong Ki. But isn't there a tong elder closer than Prescott you can call on if

70

you need to discuss something important?"

"No, Ki. There are elders in Tucson, but they are even older than I am, and the journey here is a hard one. So, since I am an old man and my days are limited, I have started to share my authority with a few of my most trusted members. Would you allow Ki to tell these few men as much as you have told me of these people who want us to join them?"

"Jessie should be the one to tell your tong members," Ki said quickly. "Not me."

Quong Ki shook his head. "This cannot be, Ki. I have gone as far as I can in asking you. There is one rule in our tong that even I cannot break. No woman may know of what we do or attend one of our meetings."

Jessie was no stranger to such restrictions; they were part of the world in which she lived and she realized that the time had not yet come to try to upset such customs.

"Ki can speak for me, Quong Ki," she said quickly. "He knows as much about them as I do."

"Will you talk to us, Ki?" the old man asked. "I promise that what you say will not be repeated."

Ki looked at Jessie and she replied with an imperceptible nod. He said, "Of course, I will. But it must be soon. Jessie wants to get back to her ranch as soon as her business here has been completed."

"By tomorrow night I can bring together the men I want to hear you," Quong Ki said. Turning to Jessie, he asked, "Will that be soon enough?"

Jessie nodded. "Tomorrow night will be fine."

"And you, Ki?" the old man went on.

Ki nodded as Jessie had and said, "I will be there; I promise you."

"I will sleep better tonight knowing that my tong has been saved from the disgrace of becoming criminals. Jessie

71

Starbuck, I am in your debt, just as I was indebted to your father. Now, let me brew fresh tea, and we will talk of other things."

As they walked to the hotel, Jessie said to Ki, "I hope I didn't ask you to do something you'd rather not face. I know the Chinese and Japanese people don't get along too well together."

"They're like oil and water," Ki said and smiled. "As a rule, they don't mix at all. Who knows, though? Perhaps his tong will find it easier to accept me because of my American blood."

A group of drunken miners in a discussion crowded the space in front of Hafford's Corner Saloon on the opposite side of the street. From the scraps of their conversation that Jessie and Ki heard it seemed to be a friendly argument that was unlikely to end in a fight, so they stopped, waiting for the men to finish talking and move on.

"Thinking of the Chinese tongs joining with the cartel makes my blood run cold," Jessie said. "I'd guess there aren't more than a few hundred cartel men in the United States right now, Ki, maybe not even that many. Why should they suddenly want more? Goodness knows, there are enough hired killers they can get to carry out their schemes."

"I'm just guessing, but it may be that the cartel's getting impatient," Ki suggested. "I don't think they've been able to carry out too many of their schemes to get a foothold in this country."

"They might have even bigger schemes in mind," she said thoughtfully. "And there are tens of thousands of Chinese in this country now. How many of them do you suppose belong to one of the tongs, Ki?"

"I wouldn't even try to guess. But the Chinese are like my own people; they feel more comfortable when they belong to some kind of organized group."

72

"Can you imagine the damage the cartel could do if it had all of the tongs working for it?"

"I can imagine it quite easily," Ki said, "and it gives me the same uneasy feeling you have."

"But why would they start in Tombstone?" she went on. "It's just a little town, Ki. Why, it's so far off the beaten track that only a few people had ever heard of it before that gunfight between the Earps and Clantons."

"Perhaps that's why, Jessie," Ki suggested. "Tombstone's had a burst of notoriety that caught public attention for a little while. Now, it'll sink back into obscurity and the cartel can operate without drawing any attention."

"We'll have to keep them from getting the tongs to work with them, Ki," Jessie went on. "Even if it means staying in Tombstone longer than we'd planned."

"If you're worried about the Circle Star, Ed and the hands can take care of things there, just as they always do when we're gone," Ki said. "Remember, Quong Ki told us there's a Western Union office just across the street from the hotel, if you want to send Ed a wire that we're going to stay here a few days longer than we'd planned."

"I just may do that tomorrow," Jessie nodded. "Then, he'll know how to reach us if something else like that poisoning business should happen. But don't you agree that we've got to stop the cartel from enlisting the tongs to help them with their dirty work?"

"Of course, I do! We've got to stop the cartel, so as soon as you finish your business with Carter, we'll start doing just that."

At last, the miners ended their argument and began to break up, drifting away singly and in groups of two or three toward their shanties. Jessie and Ki moved on to the hotel and entered its cubbyhole of a lobby. A yellow envelope stuck out of the pigeonhole bearing the number of Jessie's room. There was no one behind the registration desk, so

Ki went behind the desk and handed the envelope to Jessie.

After she'd scanned it quickly, she said to Ki, "This wire must have been delivered while we were eating. It's from Steven Carter. That meeting he had to attend is lasting longer than he'd thought it would. He won't be here until tomorrow evening."

"That gives us a free day. Do you want to spend it riding farther along the railroad right of way?"

Jessie shook her head. "No. I've seen enough to judge what the rest of it must be like. And now that I've looked at it, I'm going to sell it to Carter's syndicate. Let's spend tomorrow just looking around Tombstone, Ki. We've been here for two days now and haven't really seen anything of the town."

"Considering what we've learned tonight, that might be the wisest thing to do," Ki said. "And considering what time it is now, we'll both enjoy sleeping late tomorrow."

Jessie nodded. "Good night, then, Ki. We'll plan what to do tomorrow while we're having breakfast."

A full night's sleep in a bed rather than on a jostling train or the hard desert soil put Jessie as well as Ki in a relaxed mood. They met for breakfast the following morning.

"Did you make any plans for today?" Jessie asked when they were halfway through their meal and the edge had been taken off their hunger.

"I had a few ideas," Ki said. "But the more I thought about them, the more I realized how limited my field would be. If I talk to any of the Chinese, word that I've been asking questions would almost certainly get back to Quong Ki and might make him angry. So I decided to try the livery stables."

A frown flitted over Jessie's face, but then she nodded. "Of course. If the cartel has men here, they'd almost certainly use the same livery stable. Yes, you might get some indication of their activity that way."

"What about you?"

"Why, the bank, of course. The Starbuck name has a way of putting bank managers in a mood to talk freely. Then, I'll ride north to those smelters. The local superintendents generally know or suspect when there's anything unusual going on; they're constantly on the lookout for labor organizers. If there's time, I might even have a talk with the local marshal or whoever enforces the law here."

"Neither of us will be idle," Ki said. "And since we're having such a late breakfast, suppose we meet at the hotel for an early supper?"

Both Jessie and Ki spent longer than they'd planned on their preliminary scouting. Ki returned to the hotel first. The tiny lobby was deserted and the proprietor was not behind the registration desk, but a note was in the pigeonhole bearing the number of Jessie's room. Ki was looking at it, trying to decide whether to leave a note for her himself or go up to his room and wash up, when Jessie hurried in.

"I was afraid you'd be wondering why I'm so late getting back," she said. "Everyone I visited talked much longer than I expected."

"It seems you'll have some more talking to do this evening," Ki told her, nodding toward the note. "I'm sure you'll find that Mr. Carter has arrived to close your deal with him."

"Good," Jessie said, going behind the registration desk to take out the message and glance at it. "Yes, just as you thought, this is from Carter. He's waiting in his room until I come in, and he wants me to have dinner with him. So that will give me something to do while you're at the meeting with Quong Ki's people."

"Did you find out anything at all today?" Ki asked.

Jessie shook her head. "One or two small things. How was your luck?"

"About like yours. Nothing that can't wait until tomorrow when your railroad business is finished and we can spend all our time working together.

"I'll go to my room and clean up before I go over to Quong Ki's," Ki said. "After an afternoon visiting livery stables, I need to put on a fresh pair of sandals, at least."

"I'll do the same thing; then I'll tell Mr. Carter I'm back. He's probably wondering why he hasn't heard from me."

"We'll compare notes tomorrow," Ki said, as they walked up the stairs together. "My experience with the kind of meetings I'm going to is that they last most of the night."

In her room, Jessie undressed quickly and took a sponge bath before slipping into the one dress that she'd brought along. She went down the corridor to Carter's room and tapped on the door. Steven Carter opened it, a smile of greeting on his face.

"Miss Starbuck!" he said. "I'm sorry that I had to impose on your good nature by delaying you here in Tombstone, but I didn't have much choice, as you know."

"Please don't apologize," Jessie replied. "I've enjoyed looking around, even the rough trip along the railroad right of way. And I know the problems of staying on schedule."

"I hope you're accepting my invitation to dinner."

"Of course, I am. Ki has some business that he's attending to."

"Would you like a drink first, Miss Starbuck?" Carter asked, swinging the door open wider to show a table with a bottle of whiskey and one of sherry and the appropriate glasses.

"I think wine at dinner instead of a drink now," Jessie replied. "And please, let's stop being formal. I'm not used to being called Miss Starbuck, and I really prefer Jessie."

"Then, we'll go on at once, Jessie," he said. "And I prefer Steve to either Steven or Mr. Carter."

"Then let's have dinner, Steve."

As they went down the stairs, he said, "I've found the Maison Doree to be about the most dependable place in Tombstone to dine, so we won't have far to go."

"I've seen the sign on that restaurant downstairs," Jessie said. "And it's made me wonder a bit. It seems strange to find a French restaurant in a rough mining town such as this."

"Their French cooking has a very strong American accent," Carter said and smiled. "On my trips here since we've been interested in your railroad, I've gotten fairly well acquainted with the proprietor, who's a Scotchman by the way. But it's a step above the leathery steaks and fried potatoes or Irish stew that's about all you'll find at most of the other restaurants."

To Jessie's surprise, the dinner at the small, quiet café was very good. There was a first course of grilled mountain trout with drawn butter sauce, followed by a stuffed roasted capon, and a bottle of very palatable and properly chilled Montrachet to go with the meal. She and Carter talked very little and mostly in generalities about the mining business and its probable position in the future. When Jessie had refused a dessert and they were having black coffee, Carter lighted a cigar.

Looking at her across the table, he asked, "Shall we finish our business Jessie? I hope you've decided to sell us the railroad, now that you've seen it and can put a price on it."

"I'm not sure I can price it fairly, Steve. Suppose you make me an offer, and I'll either accept it or ask you to raise it."

"We've been thinking in terms of about forty thousand

77

dollars. After all, you don't have any rolling stock or equipment to sell."

"It would cost you twice that to build a new railroad," Jessie countered.

"And it's going to cost us twenty thousand to rebuild what we're offering to buy from you," Carter replied quickly.

"I'm not thinking in those terms," Jessie said. "I told you all I want is a fair price."

"Fifty thousand, then?"

Jessie studied Carter's expectant face a moment before she nodded and said, "That's close enough to the price I had in mind. It's yours, Steve."

"Good!" Carter smiled. "We have a deal. I was so sure we could agree that I ordered a bottle of champagne to finish off our meal."

He turned and signaled to the waiter, who disappeared for a moment and then reappeared with an ice-filled silver bucket, the neck of a bottle rising from the ice. On the serving tray beside the bucket, there were two champagne glasses. He stripped off the foil wrapper, twisted the cork until it emerged from the bottle with a gentle pop, placed the glasses on the table, and filled them. Jessie and Carter picked them up and touched their rims together, but before they could sip the wine angry voices invaded the café from the street. An instant later, two shots rang out, followed by two more.

Jessie and Carter jumped to their feet with the other half dozen diners and started toward the door. Just as Jessie stepped outside a roughly dressed man holding a revolver backed past the doorway.

A shot splintered the door jamb. The man holding the pistol grabbed Jessie by her arm and swung her body in front of his. His arm clamped her to him; then he shouted, "Throw your gun down, Behan!"

78

"You know I can't do that, Bull!" the other man called.

"Who is that you're talking to?" Jessie asked.

"It's Sheriff Behan," her captor said. "Now, you shut up till I tell you to say something!" As the man spoke, he turned his revolver and pressed it to Jessie's head. Raising his voice, he called, "You see I got her good, Behan! Now, you tell these men around me to back away. I'm going down to the OK Corral to get me a horse. Then, I'll ride outta here and nobody in Tombstone'll see me again. But don't nobody try to stop me, or this whore's gonna be dead as Mabel is!"

"Let that lady go, and I'll do what I can to help you stay clear of a hangman's noose," the sheriff shouted. "That's the best I can do for you, though!"

"Go to hell, Behan!" the man called Bull yelled.

Twisting sidewise he started moving down the street, half carrying and half dragging Jessie. He'd taken only a step or two when the sharp high-pitched bark of a small caliber weapon broke the stillness that had settled. Jessie felt her captor's body twitch and his grip suddenly grew slack. She dropped to the ground as the falling man's weapon roared and a puff of dirt spurted from the street as the slug tore into it.

Chapter 8

After the almost inaudible pop of the final shot, the small crowd outside the Maison Doree was quiet for a moment; then a burst of excited babble broke the silence.

Jessie sat up and started getting to her feet. As she rose to her knees, a hand grasped her upper arm and helped her find her balance. She looked around and saw that it was Steven Carter who had hold of her arm.

"Are you all right?" he asked.

"Of course. Nobody was shooting at me," Jessie replied calmly. She looked around. "I'd like to find whoever it was fired that last shot, though. I think he saved me from what could have been a very bad situation."

"That last shot was mine, Jessie," Carter said. Before he had a chance to go on, Sheriff Behan came up to them. He looked at Jessie and his jaw dropped.

"Miss Starbuck! When you left my office after our talk today, I didn't figure to run into you so soon again."

"And I didn't figure to see you, sheriff," Jessie said calmly.

"And I sure didn't know it was you that Bull Morgan had hold of!" Behan went on. "He didn't hurt you, did he?"

"No. But he certainly gave me a bad two or three minutes," she replied. "It's very uncomfortable to have a crazy man hold his gun to your head. But I'm sure you know that."

"Well, whoever dropped him sure did you and me both a favor," Behan said feelingly. "Bull was crazy enough so he'd've killed you for sure, and I couldn't get a bead on him without being sure I'd miss you."

"Give your thanks to Mr. Carter," Jessie told Behan. "He's the one who brought the man down."

"I owe you, Mr. Carter," Behan nodded. He looked at the group of curious bystanders crowding around the dead man and motioned for Jessie and Steve to step into the restaurant with him. Once inside, he went on, "There won't be any trouble made over your killing Bull Morgan, Mr. Carter. It had to be done."

"He acted insane, sheriff. That's why I shot him," Carter said. "I figured it was his life or Jessie's."

"Oh, Bull sorta went crazy tonight, all right," the sheriff said. "He fell hard for a new girl who came into Blond Marie's place a week or so back—wanted her to marry him and all that. She must've made him real mad tonight because he choked her to death. Marie sent one of the other girls after me, and Bull started to come peaceful, but then he knocked me down and took off running. Dazed me a minute when he hit me—he was stronger'n a bull, you know—but I got started after him before he got plumb away. Then he begun shooting."

Jessie said, "We're all lucky that it ended without a lot of people getting hurt."

"We are at that," Behan agreed. "Now, I bet you and Mr. Carter were eating your supper when all this fuss busted loose, so you just sit down and finish. I'll go outside and start taking care of things."

When the sheriff had gone, Jessie turned to Carter and said, "You offered me a drink before dinner, Steve. I think I can use it now."

"I can use one myself," he said. "But what about our champagne?"

"Right at the moment, I want something stronger," Jessie told him. "Perhaps we can have the champagne sent up to your room, and we can enjoy it after our nerves have settled down."

"An excellent idea," Carter said, picking up the bucket. "We'll make it a double celebration if you feel up to it."

"In what way?"

"I've got all the documents to close our deal in my suitcase upstairs," he explained. "The only thing that has to be done is to fill in the amount we're paying you. After we've settled our nerves with a swallow of whiskey, we can sign the papers and then celebrate with the champagne."

"That's the best idea I've heard today," Jessie replied. "What on earth are we waiting for?" As they started up the stairs, she went on, "Will you satisfy my curiosity about something, Steve?"

"Of course."

"What kind of gun are you carrying? It must be small because the bulge that a hip or shoulder holster makes is too big to be hidden by your coat. I know it's not a derringer because its report is a lot heavier than the little pop I heard."

"I'll show you when we get inside," he replied.

At the door of his room, Carter put the bucket on the floor while he unlocked the door and opened it. He stood aside for Jessie to enter, and after he'd closed the door and put the champagne on the dresser, he folded back the flap of his jacket to reveal the smallest revolver she'd ever seen. It was nestled snugly in a holster sewn inside the coat's facing a few inches above the bottom hem.

"This little gun's made in England," he went on, sliding his arms out of the sleeves. "I saw it in a gunsmith's shop in Tucson when I took my Colt in to have the trigger adjusted." After taking out the miniature revolver, he handed it to Jessie, then smiled, and added, "If you'll pardon the blunt expression, the gunsmith I bought it from called it a 'whore's gun.' Women like it because it can be hidden easily, even in the abbreviated outfits they often wear."

Jessie held the revolver in the palm of her hand, looking at it curiously. Except for its size, the pistol was an almost exact duplicate of her Colt. Its cylinder was not much bigger in diameter than her thumb. The trigger had no guard and folded upward to lie snugly against the frame below the cylinder. The barrel was about the length of her forefinger.

"It's got to be a .22," she said. "And I don't suppose it has much stopping power."

Carter looked up from the table where he was pouring their drinks and replied, "Practically none. It's only accurate up to about ten feet and has no stopping power at all. You've got to hit a vital spot with your first shot."

"Which you did and saved me from an extremely dangerous situation," Jessie observed. She stepped to the table where he was standing and laid the miniature revolver down beside the bottles. "And I don't remember whether I've even thanked you for what you did, Steve."

"I took thanks for granted," he smiled, handing her one of the glasses he'd filled.

Raising his glass, he waited for her to touch it with the rim of hers and emptied the glass with a single swallow. Jessie drank about half of the liquor in her glass, letting the smooth, aged whiskey trickle down her throat. She sat down and in a few moments felt her nerves beginning to relax.

"If you'll get out your sale agreement, Steve, I'm ready to sign it now," she said.

Nodding, Carter stepped to the suitcase that lay on the floor at the end of the bureau and took out an envelope. "I told our lawyers to make things as simple as possible," he said. "And I think you'll agree that they did."

Jessie slid the thin sheaf of papers out of the envelope

and glanced at the top page. As Carter had told her, the agreement was concise. It did not quite fill the page; the additional pages she found to be copies. Looking up at Carter, she nodded and said, "Fill in the price, Steve, and I'll sign it. Then we'll celebrate with a glass of champagne."

A bottle of ink stood on the bureau, a pen beside it. Jessie joined Steve at the bureau and for a few moments the room was silent except for the scratching of the pen. When the last copy had been signed, Steve handed two of the pages to Jessie and dropped the others into the dresser drawer.

"I'm glad we've finished our business," he said. "Now, we can drink a glass of champagne as friends without any dollar signs between us."

"They do interfere with friendship, don't they?" Jessie smiled as she followed him to the table where the champagne bucket stood, its moisture-beaded sides gleaming in the light. "Even when the people on both sides of a deal trust one another, money's a barrier between them."

"Ever since I saw you in San Antonio, Jessie, I've been wishing that barrier didn't exist. I hope you'll feel different about me now that it's gone."

"Why, I've never felt that your interest was just in money, Steve," she replied. "But we haven't seen one another often enough or for long enough to talk about our feelings."

"Isn't this a good time to start?" he asked.

"It's as good a time as any."

When Steve did not respond by taking her in his arms at once, Jessie suddenly realized that his veneer of worldliness was very thin indeed. It was shown by the obvious trouble he was having in finding the words that would carry them across the bar of a business relationship to a much more intimate one.

After a long period of solitude at the Circle Star, Jessie

re than ready to welcome a brief affair with such a
  able young man, one to whom she'd been attracted
  their first meeting. Steve's hesitation warned her now
of his inexperience, and she was afraid that if she indicated
her readiness too obviously she might drive him away. Accustomed to making quick decisions, Jessie took the risk.

"Business associates shake hands when they close a deal,"
she said. "But when one of them is a woman, don't you
think a kiss would be better?"

Jessie's frankness broke the ice. Steve took the short step
needed to bring him close to her and swept her into his
arms. Jessie lifted her lips and he found them with his. She
invited him with the tip of her tongue and he met it with
his, thrusting it deep into her mouth. His mouth covered
hers until breathlessness drove them apart, but after a few
gasping moments Steve sought Jessie's lips again. Pressing
herself to him, her hips meeting his groin, Jessie felt him
swelling.

Jessie broke their kiss to say softly, "It's not far to the
bed, and I can feel that you're as ready for it as I am."

Slowly, showing reluctance to release her, Steve led
Jessie to the bed. Jessie bent forward to blow out the lamp
on the bureau. The curtains were drawn at the windows,
but bright lamps across the street kept the room from being
completely dark. Jessie turned back to Steve at once. He'd
untied his cravat and was fumbling at his collar button.

"Let me," she said. Her nimble fingers made short work
of opening the button, and she began unbuttoning his shirt.
Jessie's fingers brushed against the soft skin at his throat,
and after the next two buttons were undone, the soft mat
of curls on his chest appeared. Their tendrils touching her
hands caused her fingers to begin trembling while she tried
to work faster.

Steve had been standing quietly until he felt the warmth

of Jessie's soft hands on his skin. He closed his palms on her waist and rested them for a moment on her hips, but when she reached his belt and began working it open, he raised his hands to her breasts and started rubbing them gently, bending to plant kisses on her soft neck.

Jessie's trembling increased. She said in an urgent whisper, "My dress opens up the back. Why don't you help me while I'm helping you?"

Steve reached around her and she felt his fingers searching for the way to release the hook-and-eye fastening that closed the placket of her dress. When he failed to master the tricky move needed to part the hooks from the little arched eyes, she stopped in the midst of unbuckling his belt and opened them herself, then slid her arms out of the sleeves, and shrugged her shoulders to let the garment slide to the floor.

With the dress out of his way, Steve easily slipped away the straps of Jessie's chemise, and it slid down over her firm high breasts. He gasped when the dim light revealed their pink rosettes, already pebbled around their protruding tips. He bent his head to caress them with his lips and tongue.

Jessie had unbuckled Steve's belt and fly when she felt the moist pressure of his lips and the flicking of his tongue on her rosettes. Involuntary shudders began sweeping through her body while she pushed Steve's trousers and underwear down over his hips where they dropped to the floor beside her dress.

Without the restraint of his underwear, Steve's swollen shaft sprang up and stood jutting between them. Jessie closed one hand around it while with the other she pushed down her silk panties and kicked them aside before rising on tiptoe and guiding the pulsing, sinewy cylinder between her thighs.

Steve's occasional trembling became constant after he

felt the warmth of Jessie's soft thighs squeezing together to cradle him, and he was shivering now, matching Jessie's anticipatory quivers. He pressed closer to her and sought her lips again, but Jessie avoided him long enough to whisper, "Don't wait, Steve! Take me to bed!"

There was no more hesitancy in Steve's movements now. He picked Jessie up and began to place her on the bed. She locked her fingers around his neck and as he lowered her to the coverlet she pulled Steve down with her. When the weight of his body pressed down on her breasts, Jessie spread her thighs wide and reached down to position his rigid shaft. She felt him going into her and locked her legs around Steve's arched back, pulling her hips up to meet his first long thrust as he drove in.

Steve's lips were seeking Jessie's now, and she turned her head to find and meet them. They pressed their mouths together, hot tongues thrusting and entwining. Jessie rocked her hips faster and Steve began stroking even more lustily. Jessie sighed gustily as she brought her rotating hips up to meet his quick short lunges, for after such a long abstinence she was already rising to a climax.

Lost to everything except the tide of passion that had both of them in its rising wave, Jessie kept her hips rocking furiously, her body quivering in its response to the quickening rhythm of Steve's stroking. Caught up urgently in their shared passion, it was difficult for them to think of anything except the climax to which they were rushing. The storm took them, and Jessie cried out as she felt herself going out of control, her world centered on the rigid cylinder of flesh that was bringing her such delight.

Steve was gasping now as he drove into Jessie's warm, encompassing moist depths. He felt her shuddering and writhing beneath him and with a few last urgent thrusts his own climax took him. He made one last deep drive before falling forward, his lips instinctively finding Jessie's, and doubly joined they lay together while the peak of their pleasure came to them and then faded slowly as their bodies went limp and they lay motionless.

Jessie was the first to recover. She sighed, a small moan smothered by the pressure of Steve's lips on hers. He lifted his head; his eyes adjusted to the dim glow that filtered into the room. Looking down at Jessie's face, a white oval framed by her touseled hair, he whispered, "There's never been a woman who's made me feel the way you do, Jessie."

"I'm glad," she replied. Then, as she felt him stir as though to get up, she tightened her thighs around his hips and held him inside her while her arms locked around his broad chest. She went on, "Don't move yet, Steve. There's still a lot of night ahead, and we don't have to hurry."

"But aren't you—"

"Tired?" she completed, anticipating his question. "No. Oh, I'm pleasantly exhausted right now, but that will pass. And I like the feeling of having you inside me."

"I like the feeling, too. But if I'm too heavy—"

"You're not. If it worries you, though, we can roll over."

"Would you like to?"

"Yes, I think I would."

Jessie locked her legs over Steve's back and closed her arms around his chest. He levered himself up, arching his hips as he moved, lifting her with him, and turned to reverse their positions. Jessie lay quietly for a few moments after they'd settled down again; then she began to work at arousing him again. Twisting her hips very slowly, she alternately tightened and relaxed her inner muscles.

Steve responded almost immediately. She felt him swelling again, and soon he was filling her once more. Lifting herself above him, Jessie began moving faster. Her breasts were swaying invitingly above her lover's face, and Steve cradled them in his cupped hands and then began rasping his tongue gently over their budded tips.

Jessie's earlier urgency had passed now. She moved slowly, stopping from time to time when she felt Steve's arousal was bringing him up too quickly. When he began thrusting upward in response to her caresses, she lay quietly. Finding his lips with hers, she held him in a tongue-entwining kiss until he lay still once more; then for a long while they lay still, Jessie's only move the alternate squeezing and relaxing of her inner muscles around Steve's engorged shaft.

She stopped even this when she felt his muscle rippling against her and lay quietly until his involuntary quivering subsided. Then, she sought his lips once more and thrust her tongue between them. Steve responded instantly. He began thrusting upward, slowly at first and then with increasing speed and force.

Jessie sensed that he'd reached the limit of his control and started jouncing her buttocks in rhythm with his thrusts, relaxing her control and racing to meet his growing frenzy. She'd almost reached her peak when Steve lifted his hips with a last fierce upward thrust.

While her lover held her impaled as he jetted in shuddering spasms, she twisted and arched her back in a few final downward strokes that brought her to her own consummation, and she relaxed on his chest while fading passion ebbed and she lay still once more.

Steve sighed after a few minutes, his breathy gust loud in the silent room. He said, "I thought I knew something about women, Jessie, but I was wrong. Do you think we can do this again after a while?"

"Of course," she said, brushing her lips over his in a soft, fleeting kiss. She lifted herself then to break the bond of flesh that had held them together so long and she cuddled beside Steve. Laying her head on his muscular chest, she added, "The night's still young. While we can, let's make the most of what we've found together."

Chapter 9

"I'm not sure I'm right, but it's certainly something we'd better look into," Jessie told Ki as they sat eating an early lunch. "I just got a quick glimpse of that man Steve shot last night, but I'm sure we've run across him before."

"One of the cartel's men?" Ki asked.

Jessie nodded and went on, "Sheriff Behan said his name was Bull Morgan, but names don't mean much where the cartel's concerned. Of course, things were happening very fast, and I was more interested in staying alive than anything else."

Jessie had already given Ki a brief account of the incident in front of the hotel the previous evening. Ki's meeting with Quong Ki and his advisers had lasted through the night, and when he'd tapped lightly on her door after reaching the hotel at daybreak, Jessie had just returned from seeing Steven Carter off on the morning stage to Tucson. She'd seen that Ki was almost as badly in need of rest as she was and suggested that they sleep through the morning and have a combined breakfast and lunch. Ki had accepted her suggestion at once.

"I can understand your desire to stay alive," Ki said. "It won't be any trouble to ask the sheriff to give us a look at the man's body."

"Looking at a corpse isn't my favorite way to start a day, but I think it's important to find out if the dead man does have a cartel connection, don't you?"

"Of course, I do, Jessie. From what I heard at Quong Ki's last night, there've been cartel men in and out of Tombstone for several months, looking over the town and trying to get him to agree on some kind of arrangement."

"But they still haven't been able to persuade him?"

Ki shook his head. "No, and I don't think they will. Only two of the six men I talked to last night wanted to make a deal with the cartel, and one of them changed his mind about it after he'd heard what I had to say. If all the tong elders are as firmly against the idea as Quong Ki, I'm sure we won't have to worry about the cartel and the tongs joining forces."

"Well, that's good news. But the cartel's going to keep on operating whether or not they get help from the tongs, Ki," Jessie said soberly.

"Of course. And we'll keep fighting them," Ki told her as he pushed his plate away. "If you're through eating, suppose we go pay a call on Sheriff Behan. We'll just about have time to catch him before he goes out to lunch."

"Well, Miss Starbuck," the sheriff said when Jessie and Ki finally reached his small office in the basement of the unfinished Cochise County Courthouse, "I wasn't looking to see you again so soon." He indicated the bare room with a sweep of his arm; it was furnished with only a small table and one chair. Behan went on, "I'd ask you to sit down, but as you see, there's no seat for me to offer you." While he was talking to Jessie, his eyes were flicking over Ki.

"We didn't come to make a long visit, sheriff," Jessie replied. "And I'm sure you've guessed it's in connection with that man who was shot last night."

"I hope you didn't suffer none," Behan said. "You just got dragged into that fracas."

"I feel fine, thank you," Jessie replied. "I don't think

94

you've met Ki yet. He's my—well, I can't describe all the jobs he does, so I'll just say he's my good right hand."

Behan nodded, but did not offer to shake hands. Following his usual custom, Ki had not extended his hand. He'd grown accustomed to the idea held by Westerners that all Orientals are servants. After several embarrassing incidents during his years with Alex when his extended hand had been ignored or taken belatedly and with reluctance, he'd adopted a quick bow on such occasions. He bowed now to Behan and brought his torso erect immediately.

"I am honored, Sheriff Behan," he said. "Jessie told me of the incident last night. It was fortunate you were close by to keep her from being harmed."

"Now, it wasn't me as much as it was Steve Carter," Behan replied. He turned to Jessie and asked, "What kind of gun was that one he tamed Morgan with? It sounded like a popgun, but it sure did do the job."

"A very small revolver," Jessie replied. "If you'd like a close look at it, stop by the hotel. Mr. Carter made me a gift of it before he left. But the reason Ki and I came to see you doesn't have any connection with the shooting, except that when I mentioned Morgan's name to Ki, he thought that he might have encountered the man before."

"I travel with Jessie," Ki volunteered. "I'm sure you know that she inherited business properties from her father, so we make frequent inspection trips together."

"I see," Behan said. "I guess Miss Starbuck told you what I said about Morgan not being that fellow's real name?"

"Yes. And the thought occurred to both of us that if you know his real identity you might want to notify some of your law enforcement colleagues that he's dead. It would save them the trouble of continuing to look for him."

"Now, that's right thoughtful of you and Miss Starbuck, Ki. I looked through all my Wanted posters this morning, and there were two or three that fit his description, but none of the names on them was his." Behan paused long enough to light a cigar and then went on, "If you want to look at him, it won't be no trouble. I got him tucked away at Gird's Ice Plant till we can get him buried. It's just a block up the street from here."

They picked their way to Toughnut Street through a litter of boards, stacks of stone blocks, and sacks of cement, and they dodged a dozen workers bustling around the slowly rising walls. Behan led them past rows of small miner's cabins toward Fifth Street and a pair of squat adobe buildings on the corner.

Circling the buildings, they followed the sheriff to the smaller one. He opened its door. As warm air entered, a mist rolled out and obscured the interior. Then, the fog dissolved and they saw the bulky body of the dead man lying on a canvas tarpaulin atop the big blocks of ice that filled the small squat storage building.

Ki and Jessie looked at the body for a moment, then consulted one another using small nods and a brief flicking of their eyebrows.

Jessie said, "I'm sure that's the same man I saw some time ago a little way from Carson City. Am I right, Ki?"

"Yes," Ki agreed. "But he was going under a different name then, if you remember. Slip Johnson, he called himself."

"Of course," Jessie said. Turning to Behan, she went on, "And I'm positive it's the same man, sheriff."

"Did you have trouble with him that time?" Behan asked.

"He was causing trouble for everyone," Jessie replied. "It was during a dispute between a little town up there and a new railroad. They'd hired some rough characters, and he was one."

"Sure sounds like Bull," Behan said. "He's been in and

96

out of hot water ever since he got here. He wasn't in town more than a few days before he started hanging out with a rough bunch down at the Silver Rail Saloon."

"I don't think he'd have remembered me," Jessie went on. "And I doubt if that was why he grabbed me last night. All he wanted was someone to put between you and him, sheriff. He'd have taken hold of anybody."

"I'm sure that's right, Jessie," Ki agreed. "And now that you've satisfied your curiosity about having seen that fellow before, shall we be getting on our way?"

"You've been real helpful, Miss Starbuck," Behan said as Jessie and Ki started to leave. "If you need anything I can help you with while you're here, be sure to let me know."

As they left the ice storage shed and started walking toward Toughnut Street, Jessie told Ki, "If we weren't sure about the cartel's plans before, we certainly don't have to guess any longer."

"No," Ki replied thoughtfully. "Those few minutes with Sheriff Behan were very rewarding. We know now where to look for the cartel's local headquarters."

"Don't you think we should give the Silver Rail a bit of unobtrusive attention on our way back to the hotel?" Jessie asked.

"Just what I was going to suggest."

"Do you know where it is, Ki?"

"No. But I have an idea that if we just walk up Fifth Street we'll find it without much trouble. From the way Sheriff Behan spoke when he mentioned the Silver Rail, my hunch is that it'll be in or close to the red light district."

"We won't have far to walk," Jessie said.

They walked unhurriedly up Fifth Street to Allen and turned toward the cluster of wooden buildings that had been the nucleus of Tombstone's original settlement. As they passed a Wells Fargo office and the Arizona Brewery and approached the Birdcage Theatre, they could see the first of the red lanterns hanging over the doors at the beginning of the district. About half the lanterns were lighted, though their glass shades glowed dimly in the bright noonday sun.

Ki pointed to a sign on Sixth Street as they came to a halt at an intersection. "There's the Silver Rail, just beyond that long building on the corner," he said. "There aren't many people around, but I don't think we'd attract any attention if we were to walk past it to see if we can get a glimpse inside."

"It's too bad I don't have on a flashy dress and hat," Jessie remarked as they passed a woman in the intersection. She was wearing a garish dress of purple satin and a hat heavy with an arrangement of flowering twigs on which a pair of stuffed birds were perched. "I'd look just like I belonged here, and nobody would notice me."

Ki smiled as he replied. "You draw attention everywhere you go, Jessie, and what you happen to be wearing has nothing to do with it."

"I suppose I can take that as a compliment," she said. "If it is, thank you, Ki."

They fell silent as they reached the Silver Rail. The saloon was one of the older buildings in the area. It was a wooden two-story structure badly in need of paint. The windows on the upper floor were tightly shuttered, and as far as they could tell from the glimpse they got of its sides, there were no openings on the first floor except the swinging doors in front. Jessie and Ki had been walking very slowly; now they slowed their pace still further.

When they came abreast of the saloon, the doors were closed and motionless; all they could do was look inside through the wide gap between the bottom of the door and the floor, and all they saw was a miscellaneous array of booted feet strung out along the bar. They'd almost passed the Silver Rail when a door across the street slammed with a bang loud enough to draw their attention to the woman who'd come out of it.

She hurried across the street at an angle that would take her to the door of the saloon. She was wearing the abbreviated costume of her profession: a knee-length red satin dress trimmed with wide blue lace along the low-cut bodice and hemline, sheer full-length hose that disappeared under the skirt and high-heeled patent leather shoes. A lace shawl over her head shielded her face and hid her hair. She passed Jessie and Ki close enough for them to get a whiff of an overpowering perfume before she ran up the steps of the saloon and pushed through the doors.

"Too bad we'd already passed that door," Ki commented. "If we'd been about a minute later, we'd have been able to get a glimpse inside."

"I think the boots along the bar told us enough to imagine what it's like," Jessie said. "They weren't miner's boots, Ki. They were the kind of boots worn by men who spend most of their time on horseback."

"But since we recognized that dead man as a cartel man, there might have been some more familiar faces in there," Ki pointed out.

"Yes. But there's a good chance they might've recognized us, too," Jessie reminded him.

"You're right, of course," Ki said. "Though if the cartel bosses haven't learned we're in Tombstone yet, it won't be very long before they find out."

They'd reached Fremont Street by now and turned toward the center of town. Walking faster, they came to the intersection of Fifth Street, and Jessie glanced at the small display windows of Dillon & Keanely's General Store. An array of multicolored bolts of cloth drew her eye and she slowed down to look at them. As she gazed at the brilliant fabrics, a scheme burst into her head. She thought about it, elaborating on the original germ of thought as they crossed Fifth Street, and by the time they'd turned to get back to the hotel, she turned to Ki.

"I've just had an idea," she said. "We're fairly sure we know what the cartel's planning, but it would certainly help us a lot if we knew the details."

"Of course, it would. What do you have in mind?"

"Getting inside the Silver Rail where I can hear what the cartel's hirelings are talking about."

Ki stopped and stared at her, surprise as well as consternation mingling on his usually expressionless face. After a moment he asked, "Are you serious, Jessie?"

"I certainly am."

"Suppose you tell me exactly what your plan is."

"That girl who went into the Silver Rail when we were passing it must hear a lot of unguarded talk, Ki. She probably doesn't know what most of it means and doesn't care, but it would be valuable information for us."

"Are you suggesting that we bribe her to tell us what she hears?"

"I'm sure we could," Jessie nodded. "But I'm not at all sure that she could understand what kind of information is important to us. We'd run the risk of her overlooking something vital, and there's always the chance that she'd sell us out."

"Where does that leave us?"

"With me. All I need is the clothes."

Ki controlled his expression this time, but his voice gave away his concern. "You, Jessie? Dressing like a saloon girl and eavesdropping at the Silver Rail? No, indeed!"

"I'm the only one who can do it, Ki," she said quietly.

"It's too dangerous," Ki said. His voice was under control

by now. He went on, "Suppose one of the cartel's gunslingers recognizes you?"

"I don't think there are many left alive who've ever seen me, Ki," Jessie replied. "At least not at close range. Right across from our hotel there's a barber shop; they have a sign that they sell hair goods, so I'll get a black wig. And I'll be wearing so much rouge and lipstick that there won't be much chance I'll be recognized—even by somebody who knows me."

"Please, Jessie, don't even think about doing anything as risky as that," Ki said.

"I've already thought about it, Ki," she answered calmly, "and it's the only way I can see that we're going to find out what the cartel has in mind before they get into action. If we wait, it'll be too late for us to move effectively."

Ki recognized the finality in Jessie's tone. Only rarely did she exercise the authority both of them were aware was hers. Usually she maintained the relationship that they'd established soon after Alex's death—partners sharing a job and discussing their moves in detail before acting. This time, however, Jessie's words and tone made it clear to Ki that she'd made her decision and her plan was not open for discussion. Still, he decided to make one final try.

"What about the clothes you'll need?" he asked. "It'll take you several days to find someone to make your dress and get you the things like the wig that you'll need to go with it."

"I've thought of that, too," she said. "We'll go back to the district and I'll find a girl near enough my size who'll sell me a—" Jessie hesitated. "Well, I suppose you'd call them a set of her working clothes."

Ki gave up. "Since you've made up your mind, I won't object," he told her. "Let's go."

At the corner of Sixth Street, Jessie stopped and said, "I

don't think you'd better come with me any farther, Ki. This is something I need to do alone. It shouldn't take me very long. Suppose you wait for me here."

Ki nodded and watched Jessie as she crossed the street and stopped. Jessie studied the arrangement, shook her head almost imperceptibly, then went toward the most imposing of the three or four houses, and vanished from Ki's sight.

Jessie realized that it made very little difference which door she tried. She rapped at the first door and after a moment it was opened by a flamboyantly dressed blonde who might have been any age between twenty and forty.

She wore a white dress, its skirt as short as the one worn by the woman who had crossed the street, and high black stockings. Her hair was piled in a pompadour; her face was heavily made up. She looked at Jessie for a moment, her lips curling disdainfully.

"One of those, eh?" she said and then added quickly, "Well, come on in. I don't mind obliging you, but it's going to cost you double."

"I'm not looking for your services," Jessie said quickly. She'd sized up the woman at a glance and saw that they were near enough in size so she'd be able to wear her clothes. "I want to buy one of your dresses and whatever else goes with it."

"Listen, honey, if you're in the life and wanta get set up here, you'll have to go talk to—"

"No, no!" Jessie broke in. "I want it for a disguise." Then, she added quickly, "At a masquerade party."

"Oh, I get it," the blonde nodded. "Well, come on in. I guess I can find something you can use."

Until the door closed behind her, Jessie hadn't realized how small the little room was. It was furnished with a double bed, a chair, and a table on which stood a washbowl and

102

pitcher. The bed was almost as wide as the room, and there was barely enough clearance between the foot of the bed and the two pieces of furniture for a person to squeeze in. Heady perfume permeated the air.

Tossing back the crumpled bedspread, the woman dragged out a large suitcase from under the bed and opened its lid. Silken garments were mixed in the bag, a wild scramble of brilliant rainbow colors.

"Take your pick, honey," she said. "Red, green, purple, orange, pink, or yellow."

Jessie lifted the tangled mass of silk and saw that there were two red dresses. She picked up one of them and said, "I'll take this one. And I'll need stockings. And under-clothes."

For a moment the woman stared at Jessie, her mouth open with astonishment. She chuckled and said, "My gawd, you've been telling me the truth!" Lifting her skirt, she exposed her torso up to her waist. Except for straps that supported her hip-high stockings, she wore nothing under the dress. She went on, "Us girls in the life ain't got time to waste taking down our pants and pulling 'em up again, lady. If you got to have a pair of drawers, you'll have to use your own."

"All right," Jessie said quickly. "How much do you want for the dress and stockings?"

"Even if I figure you can afford it, I ain't got the heart to stick an innocent like you, honey," the woman replied. "The stockings cost me a dollar and the outfit was six when it was new, which it ain't now. Take both of 'em for five."

Silently, Jessie took five dollars from her purse and stuffed the dress and hose inside. "Thank you," she said. "You've been very honest with me."

"Ah, hell! Forget it! And have a good time at your dance or whatever it is you're going to."

103

After hurrying through the alley to Sixth Street, Jessie joined Ki at the corner. He looked at her questioningly when he saw that she was not carrying a package.

"Don't worry," she said, "I've got what I went after in my purse. Now, let's get back to the hotel and make some plans."

"We'd better make careful plans," Ki said as they started down Fremont Street. "I have some uneasy feelings about this scheme, Jessie."

"I'm doing the only thing possible in this situation, Ki," Jessie said. "And even if something goes wrong, you'll be close by to give me a hand. Now, stop worrying!"

Chapter 10

"You'd better take one last look at me now, Ki," Jessie said as she stopped in the light that spilled from the windows of a store. "The street's dark as pitch ahead, so I want to be sure I look all right."

As she turned around, Ki inspected her and said, "You look just like what you're made up to be, Jessie. And with that black wig on, even if you run into somebody who's seen you before, I don't think he'd recognize you."

"Does my little pistol show?" she asked, lifting her left arm and peering down herself to inspect the slight bulge the .22 made in the holster she'd improvised from a scrap of cloth. She'd sewn it just below her armpit in the bodice of her sleeveless dress.

Ki shook his head. "Anyone who didn't know it was there wouldn't notice it. But I still wish you wouldn't take such a risk."

"I'm not going to give up my plan now," Jessie replied.

Ki recognized the determination in her voice and said only, "I'll be across the street watching."

"I'll feel better knowing that," she said. "Now, let's go on to the Silver Rail. It's early yet, but I want to have a chance to look around before the place gets too busy."

Silently, they moved on to the corner and turned down Sixth Street. All the red lanterns were glowing now. They gave the street very little light, but did impart an unearthly glow to their surroundings. Halfway to the Silver Rail, Ki angled across the street and took up the position he and Jessie had agreed on—in the dark narrow gap between two of the parlor houses. He turned and watched Jessie as she entered the saloon, and then he hunkered down for what he hoped would be a short wait.

Jessie walked jauntily into the saloon. She blinked to clear her eyes after she entered. Not only was the bar room brighter than the street, but a veil of bluish smoke swirled above the bar, veiling the oil lamps that hung from the ceiling. Jessie stepped to one side of the door and stood in the quiet corner opposite the long bar for a moment. She let her eyes adjust from the darkness of the street.

There were fewer than a dozen men standing at the bar, which stretched from just inside the entrance almost to the back of the narrow room. A half dozen small square tables hugged the wall on the side where Jessie stood, and in a clear space beyond the end of the bar there were chuck-a-luck and faro tables. Neither of the tables was in operation, and there were no signs of the gamblers who ran the games.

Jessie wondered if she'd gotten there too early, for at the moment she was the only woman in the place. Few of the drinkers gave her more than a cursory glance as she made her way to the rear, still swinging her hips provocatively. The drinkers at the bar paid little attention to her. Three or four of them turned to look as she passed, but none of them gave her more than a quick glance.

Jessie started for the last of the small tables lined up against the wall, but before she reached it one of the bar-keeps signaled her to come over.

"I guess you're the new girl?" he inquired, staring at her closely. "Betty? Belle? Something like that."

Jessie realized she was being handed an opportunity. "Belle," she said. "My first night here."

106

"Slats must've forgot to tell me you'd got in," the man said. "He laid out the deal for you, didn't he?"

"You mean the pay?" Jessie guessed, hoping her stab in the dark was correct.

"That's right."

"He talked a lot of figures, but maybe I've forgotten some of them," she replied.

"All right, Belle, just see you remember 'em this time," the barkeep said. "You get two bits out of every dollar when you're shilling a customer. Twenty percent if you get him to buy a bottle to take with you across the street. What're you getting for a trick? A half a buck or a buck?"

"Whichever I can get easiest," Jessie said, grabbing her answer out of thin air again.

"That figures," the man nodded. "We knock off a dime from your tab for every dollar trick. Settle up when you quit for the night. Whatever you make on tricks who go to your place without us sending them, you keep. After you turn a trick, you bring the customer over here whenever you can, and if he spends three dollars or more, you're paid double. Now, you got all that down so you won't forget it again."

She nodded. "I'll remember it this time."

"Oh, yeah," the barkeep went on, "there's a couple of things I forgot myself. I guess Slats told you about the chips?"

"He said something about them, but I was real sleepy and I might've got it mixed up," Jessie improvised again.

Digging under his apron, the man brought out a poker chip in which an X had been scored into one side with the tip of a knife. "When we send a trick over to you with one of these, you don't charge him. Just pass the chip back to us and we pay you. Get it?"

Thinking fast, Jessie was positive she saw the point.

"Sure," she replied, "and I don't collect anything from him but the chip."

"You damned well better not try to charge the trick, unless you want to get that pretty face of yours busted up," he stated. "And you better remember what Slats told you about the upstairs."

Glancing around, Jessie saw no sign of a stairway. She asked, "Where's the stairs? Slats didn't show me."

"Up in front," he told her. "But that's not any of your business. In this place you don't work upstairs; you take your tricks across the street. Just steer clear of that second floor unless me or Slats or Ritter invites you up, and you'll do all right here."

Jessie caught herself just in time to keep from asking who Ritter was. Instead, she replied, "Don't wory. I'll play by the rules."

"Good," the barkeep said. "Now, you got time to turn a trick or two before the place gets crowded. If you run into trouble, just yell. We'll see you don't get hurt; that's one reason you're working here instead of by yourself."

"Thanks," Jessie said, "but there's one thing you forgot to tell me."

"What the hell is that?"

"Your name."

"Hey, you're all right, Belle," the man said. "I'm Ernie. And if I come knocking on your door one morning before too long, don't you be surprised."

"I won't," Jessie said. Then, to keep in character, she added, "You're all right yourself, Ernie."

"We'll get along," the man said and nodded. "But if you're going to work the bar for a few drinks and maybe pick up an early trick or two, you better get moving."

"Sure," Jessie said. Then she dropped her voice and went on, "Look, Ernie, I guess I'm a little bit nervous, this being

108

my first night here. I've got to go, but I don't know where the privy is."

"Outside and around the corner of the building. It's just a one-holer, so get in and out of it quick as you can," Ernie said as he motioned toward a side door.

"Thanks," Jessie said. "I'll only be a minute."

She found the door and tried the knob. It turned easily and she pushed the door open and slipped through. A stairway was visible for only a brief moment, and she reopened the door a crack to let light from the bar trickle in. By its dim gleam she saw an enclosed stairway that had been built on one wall of the building the Silver Rail occupied, a stairway that gave no hint of its existence because of its placement between the outer saloon wall and the outer wall of the building that housed the saloon.

Another door was visible now. Jessie crossed to it and tried the knob. It opened easily. She felt a rush of cool outdoor air and saw a triangle of sky at the top of the doorway. After closing it and the door that led to the saloon, Jessie stood in total darkness until she could pierce the black gloom. Then, she started feeling her way up the stairs.

With each step the darkness increased until she had covered the first steps. Then, a glow showed from above. Jessie had gotten her night vision now. She moved a bit faster, and as she drew closer to the light, she saw that the glow was coming from a thin crack at the bottom of a door at the head of the stairway.

Pressing one hand against the wall and stepping slowly, carefully, and noiselessly on the bare wooden steps, Jessie continued up the stairway. The door at the top was unlocked, and she opened it slowly. A narrow hall was on the other side and Jessie stepped into it, closing the door behind her. One side of the passageway she entered was blank, broken only by a bracket holding a lamp, its wick turned so low that it barely glowed. The opposite side of the hall was broken by a series of four doors.

Jessie went to the first door and pressed her ear against it. She listened for a moment, while the sounds of her breathing seemed to increase in the silence, but she heard neither voices nor movement. Trying the knob, Jessie discovered that the door was locked and moved on to the next one. Again, her careful listening was rewarded only by silence, and after trying the knob and finding it was also locked, she moved to the third door.

When she pushed her ear against its panel, Jessie was sure she heard some kind of muted sounds, but they were so faint that she could not identify them. She was reaching for the knob to try opening the door when she heard the distant thudding of a door being closed, followed by the sound of footsteps mounting the stairs.

Without trying any longer to move silently, Jessie grabbed the knob of the door in front of her and twisted it hard. To her surprise, the knob turned readily and she pushed the door open. It was illuminated by an unshaded lamp that stood on a table in the center of the room. She saw a closed door in the wall to her right and started to go to it, but the footfalls on the stairs were growing louder, telling her that her time was running out.

Even though Jessie realized that she'd already seen everything the room contained, she looked around again, trying to think of a way to use the table for cover, knowing as she looked that it was hopeless. The opened door to the hall caught her eye, and as she hurried to close it, to gain another second or two. She heard the door to the stairway open.

As she quickly swung the door of the room closed, Jessie saw one way that she might stay hidden for at least a few seconds more. The footsteps of the person who'd just come up the stairs were reverberating in the hall now. Swinging around, Jessie pressed herself against the wall as close as possible to the door, where the door itself would shield her once it was opened.

Only seconds passed before the footsteps in the hall stopped abruptly. The doorknob grated and the door swung open. Through the crack between the edge of the door and its frame, Jessie saw the glint of glass and metal and beyond them a thin slice of the figure of a man moving past the crack as he entered the room. He stopped beside the table and Jessie heard a muted metallic thud followed by the clinking of glass.

Pressed into the tiny area between the wall and the opened door which concealed her, Jessie stood still while the faint sounds from the table continued. The click of a doorknob being turned overrode the faint tinklings from the table; another person entered and then a man's voice broke the silence.

"Sorry it took me so long to bring up these drinks you wanted," the first man said. "We had a big rush downstairs and I had to stay and give Ernie a hand."

"It's all right," the other man answered.

Jessie knew the voice; it grated like a file scraping on hard metal and it belonged to a man named Ritter. He was one of the minor lieutenants of the cartel who had been in California, and though she and Ki had defeated Ritter's gang, the fight had been a bitter one.

Raising his voice, Ritter went on, "We finally got the drinks. You fellows come in and help yourselves. I'm damned if I'm going to play barkeep for you."

A babble of more distant voices replied, so mixed that Jessie could not separate them. Chair legs scraped and footsteps thunked on bare wood. Then, Ritter's voice overrode the lesser sounds as he said, "You better get back downstairs, Lopez. You said the place was busy."

111

"Yes, Mr. Ritter."

Jessie recognized the voice as that of the man who'd brought up the liquor. She heard his footsteps on the floor and glimpsed him moving past the crack of the door, but even before he'd gone, the men to whom Ritter had called were moving into the room. They were talking among themselves, but their voices were so low that the thudding of their feet on the bare floorboards, the tinkling of glasses, and the garbled words of their conversation as they gathered around the table made it impossible for Jessie to catch more than a few meaningless words of their brief exchanges. They fell silent after a few confused moments and Ritter spoke again.

"You men want to go back in the other room where we can sit down?" he asked. "We can carry the liquor in there where we'll be a little bit more comfortable."

"I'm glad to get a chance to stand up," a new voice responded. "Tombstone's a hell of a long way from anyplace, and between trains and stagecoaches I've about had my fill of sitting down."

"Whatever the rest of you want to do is good enough for me," a third man said.

"I feel like Blake does," another remarked. "Standing up feels pretty good."

Jessie marked the name Blake. She supposed he was one of the cartel bosses of whom she'd not yet heard.

"Whatever we say, we'll just be talking in circles until Schneider and the Count get here," Blake told his companions. "And both of them are going to want some answers about why we haven't made any better progress."

Again, Jessie added to her mental list. She'd heard of the man called the Count before; he was an authentic nobleman of a poverty-stricken line, while Schneider was obviously a high-ranking cartel member whose name she hadn't heard before.

112

Ritter spoke again. "Schneider's just like all the others who've never been in this part of the country. He doesn't understand that it's not just a neat little package like ones in Europe. The Count's a little better; he's seen more."

During the brief pause that followed, Jessie thought furiously. Except for the Count and Ritter, all the names she'd heard mentioned were strange to her. She realized from what they'd said that she'd stumbled into a meeting of the cartel's leaders, and from Ritter's last remark she deduced that the cartel's European bosses were coming because there was some dissatisfaction with the slow progress the sinister group was making in taking over Tombstone and its mineral riches.

"When will Schneider be here?" The voice was that of one of the men for whom she had no name, but she got one when Ritter answered his question.

"He's supposed to be here by now, Furnas. So is the Count. But I haven't had any word from either of them."

"They're not going to be happy at the slow progress we've been making," Furnas said. "I suppose we'd better go back and sit down and see if we can make up another timetable."

"Good enough," Ritter replied. "Bring whatever bottles you want and we'll go sit down again. But first, I'll just close this door."

Before Jessie could think of any kind of move, the door that had shielded her was jerked away and she stood facing the stares of four men who were as surprised as she was.

Jessie's reactions were fast, but not as fast as Ritter's. She brought up her right hand, reaching for the pistol hidden under her left arm, but Ritter grabbed her wrist with a speed she hadn't anticipated and then grasped her left arm at once. Jessie aimed a kick at his crotch, but Ritter pulled her away from the wall just as she lifted her foot from the floor. She swung to one side and her upthrusting knee slid off his thigh.

"Stand still, damn you!" Ritter said as he twisted Jessie's arms together with strong, merciless hands and pushed them downward, forcing Jessie to bend forward.

She tried in vain to free her wrists, but Ritter's hands were big and the bowed position into which he'd pushed her limited severely the free use of her legs and feet. When he began backing toward the table, forcing her to move with him or be dragged across the floor, Jessie realized that for the moment further struggling would be useless, so she hobbled along with Ritter as he began pulling her away from the wall.

"Who the hell is she?" Blake asked.

"One of the girls from the saloon downstairs," Ritter replied. "All of them wear the same kind of outfits, and I haven't been able to get a good enough look at her face to tell which one she is."

Jessie kept her back bowed and her face hidden even as Ritter reached the table. When he yanked at her wrists to pull her erect, she bowed her head to prevent him from getting a clear view of her face. Even when he increased his pressure on her wrists and forced her to straighten up, Jessie kept her head bowed.

"Stand up straight!" Ritter snapped. "I want a good look at you!"

Jessie kept her head down in spite of the almost paralyzing pains that by now were shooting up her arms.

Furnas stepped behind her and thrust his fingers into Jessie's wig. He pulled and the wig came away in his hand.

"Hell, she's not one of the saloon girls!" Ritter exclaimed. "She's some kind of damned spy!"

Furnas dropped the wig and this time he buried his fingers in Jessie's own hair and yanked with a merciless jerk that forced her to lift her chin.

"Well, I'm damned!" Ritter exclaimed. "We've got ourselves a real prize here! This dame is Jessie Starbuck!"

"Jessie Starbuck," Furnas said gleefully. "Well, what do you think of this?" he called, addressing Greener, the man who stood at the doorway.

"What a nice surprise you guys planned for my arrival!" said Greener, another cartel honcho.

Chapter 11

Hunkered down in the deep shadow between two parlor houses across the street from the Silver Rail, Ki quelled his misgivings as he waited and watched the saloon. It was a slow night in Tombstone.

When his well-trained muscles began to complain and show the first signs of becoming cramped, Ki shifted his position a bit to relieve them and then settled down to continue his vigil.

Ki had no way of knowing that Jessie was sitting uncomfortably, facing the four cartel men who'd captured her. A hastily rolled bandanna held her hands behind her lashed to the back of a chair, and another had been used as a gag.

Since the gag had been put on her mouth, Jessie had been studying her four captors. She'd learned soon after the beginning of her battle against the cartel that there was a great deal of difference between its key men.

Ritter looked like he might have worked as a ranch foreman before joining the cartel. He was a stocky man, his face was deeply tanned, and he had a square clean-shaven jaw. His eyes were hard and his hands big, bearing evidence that they'd once been callused from hard physical work. His voice was like a rasp, the voice of a man accustomed to shouting orders, and he had the manner of one who expected to be obeyed.

Blake, on the other hand, was tall and slight. He wore

a well-trimmed mustache that had the effect of making his narrow face seem broader than it really was. His voice was low. It was a cultured voice, that of a man of wealth who did not need to speak above a conversational tone to get attention. He was the only one of the four who wore a business suit, a style of dressing that was more appropriate to the offices of a brokerage house or a bank than to a rough mining town like Tombstone. Only his eyes gave him away; they were serpent's eyes, cold and hard.

Both Furnas and Greener had the faded rusty complexion of men who had once worked outdoors, but were now confined to an office desk. Of the two, Furnas was the most self-assured. His clipped speech indicated a good education, and he moved with the swift, assured moves of an athlete. His face was neutral; it would have gone unnoticed in a crowd except for his mouth. It was virtually lipless, a thin straight line that when closed made him appear to have no mouth at all.

Greener had the big hands of a farmer and the slightly stooped shoulders of a man once accustomed to bending forward while he worked. His oval face was expressionless except when he knitted his heavy brows, and then his light blue eyes squinted as though he needed to concentrate on every word in order to understand. He was stockily built and his rumpled suit fitted him badly.

Jessie had lost track of how much time had passed since they'd subdued her and tied her up, but having been held prisoner on other occasions, she was sure it hadn't been as long ago as it seemed. So far, she'd done nothing but stare in stony silence at them. For a while, the group had tried to question her, but she'd acted as though they hadn't spoken, and in angry disgust Ritter had ordered them to gag her.

"She's a stubborn bitch, Ritter," Furnas said after he'd

finished knotting the bandanna around Jessie's mouth. "We're going to have to use a little bit more persuasion."

"What've you got in mind?"

"I never met a good-looking woman who didn't open up when I held a lit cigar up close to the tip of her tits and told her that if she didn't start talking I'd move it the rest of the way," Furnas replied. "And there are a few more things that work if the cigar doesn't tame her."

"Our friend Furnas is right," Blake agreed. "We're wasting time here."

"Just keep your pecker in your pants," Ritter advised them. "We don't want to make any sort of move right now. First of all, I haven't had a word from Schneider or the Count for a while. They might not like it if we do anything about the Starbuck woman before they can ask her some questions."

Greener broke in to ask, "How in hell can they expect to get her to talk if we can't?"

"Suppose you ask them," Ritter shot back. "Schneider's got some real mean ways of getting people to talk, and from what I hear about the Count, he's meaner than Schneider. Both of them being up with the big bosses, I say we'd better play it safe."

"What are we going to do?" Furnas asked. "Just sit here and roll our thumbs and wait?"

"Wait, maybe," Ritter said, "but not here. It took us a long time to get our hands on the Silver Rail, and we need it to go on with what we plan to do with this town. I don't intend to be the one who gets the blame for losing it."

"Who'd want this town?" Greener asked.

Ritter pointed at Jessie and said, "She would, for one, if you give her half a chance."

"Hell, she's nothing but a woman!" Furnas snorted.

"She's more like a puma and a rattlesnake rolled up into

one," Ritter shot back. "And if Jessie Starbuck's in Tombstone, it's dollars to doughnuts that her damn Chinee is here, too. He's almost as bad medicine as she is. I had a brush with them out in California one time that cost me some good men, and I know what I'm talking about."

"Why haven't we got rid of them?" Greener asked.

"If you'd been with us longer, you'd know why," Blake put in. "Just take Ritter's word for it, those two are poison. They've pulled some stunts that're hard to swallow."

If Jessie's mouth had not been gagged, she would have smiled in spite of her precarious situation. The discussion she'd just heard between the cartel men told her that the battles she and Ki had fought with the sinister group since Alex's death had shaken its members badly. But she had also hoped to hear mention of Bannon and the poison and what connection he had to the cartel.

Ritter said to Greener, "Now that you're this close to the top, you've got a right to know a few things. Schneider's the one who's supposed to tell them to you, but I'll give you a few hints to go on. We've got to keep the Starbuck woman alive until he gets here because we want everything her father left her, and it'll be easier to get it if she's alive than it would be without her help."

"From what I've seen, we don't have a chance of getting her to help us," Greener objected.

"If Schneider can't get her to cooperate, then the Count can have her. From what I've heard about him, she won't be good for anything but a bullet by the time he gets through with her."

For the first time since she'd been taken by the cartel men, Jessie began to worry. She had no doubt that Ritter was telling his cohorts the truth, and the thought that she might aid the cartel in spite of herself sent a chill up her spine.

"That sounds real good," Greener said. "But what are we going to do with her until Schneider and the Count get here?"

"Well, we've got her safe right now," Blake observed. "We can just keep her here in the Silver Rail."

Ritter shook his head. "Too dangerous," he said. "We haven't got this town sewed up tight yet. For one thing, I've got a pretty good idea that old Quong Ki's not going to throw in with us. He didn't come right out and say no when I talked to him this afternoon, but he didn't say yes, either."

"From what I heard last, you had it set up so he'd split the town with us," Blake said.

"I thought so," Ritter said curtly. "But it looks as if he's changed his mind. So we're going to need more men than we'd figured on."

"We've got them," Furnas said. "All we have to do is get them here, and that won't take more than a week or two."

"It still means we've got to change some of our plans," Ritter said curtly. "There's a lot of people we've got to get rid of so we can put our own men in the jobs they've got now. Tombstone's gotten so big since we first began planning our move that it's going to take us longer than we'd expected."

As she listened to the confident explanations Ritter was giving his gang, Jessie's anger and anxiety increased. She was sure that Ki would find a way to free her sooner or later, but what she'd heard had made her start wondering if he could get to her in time to thwart the cartel's ambitious scheme.

"That means we can't keep the Starbuck woman at the Silver Rail, I guess," Furnas said. "What'll we do with her while we're waiting for Schneider and the Count?" Furnas asked Ritter.

121

"I've got that figured out, too," Ritter said. "The best place we can take her is to the hide-out we fixed up when we first began taking over Tombstone. It's out in the mountains a few miles to the east."

"Isn't there somewhere here in town we could keep her?" Blake asked. "I've done enough traveling just to get here, and I don't enjoy horseback riding in rough country."

"I guess you can stay behind if you want to," Ritter said coldly. "Of course, Schneider might wonder why you didn't go along to help us."

"Never mind, Ritter," Blake replied hurriedly. "I'll go with you. When do we start?"

"We'll want to leave here an hour or so after midnight," Ritter replied. "There won't be many people stirring around to notice us then, and by the time we get close to the old hide-out it'll be light enough so we can see where we're going over the roughest part of the trail."

"Are we just going to keep her up there until we leave?" Furnas asked.

"I don't see why not," Ritter said and shrugged. "She's tied up good, and she won't do any yelling if we leave her gagged. There's no windows for her to get out, and we can lock the doors. Nobody but me has the keys."

"Don't you think one of us ought to stay and keep an eye on her?" Greener suggested.

"I don't see that we need to," Ritter replied. "The main reason the three of you are here is for me to show you our first targets and get you acquainted with the town. Once we start rolling on this job, I want it to go smoothly without anybody messing up."

"Well, you know the setup better than we do," Blake said, "so if we're going to look at the town, let's get started."

With the patience that came from the Japanese half of his heritage, Ki had kept himself still and had not even changed

122

his position greatly since Jessie went into the Silver Rail. In spite of his growing concern for Jessie's safety, he'd moved only to take what his martial arts training had taught him was a necessary precaution; he had changed his posture and moved about a bit from time to time in order to keep his muscles from becoming cramped.

He'd risen to his feet and stretched and was taking short strides in the deep gloom between the two parlor houses when he glanced across at the saloon. As fleeting as his look had been, Ki had gotten a glimpse of shadowy forms almost totally invisible in the dense blackness at one side of the building. Knowing from past experience that those who move in darkness are generally up to no good, he decided to investigate.

Deep blackness draped the street. The darkness was relieved only by the dim red glow of the lanterns and the slivers of light that streamed from the spaces above and below the saloon's front door. It was an easy job for Ki to cross the street. He used *ninjitsu*, crawling and rolling, staying in the dense spots where his dark blouse and loose black trousers would be unseen.

In spite of Ki's swift moves, he did not reach the opposite side of the street before the men had walked around to the front of the Silver Rail and stopped at the rail in front of the saloon. Ki stopped at the edge of the lighted area and froze, blending with the darkness. He was close enough to the four men to hear them and he strained to catch the words of the one who was speaking.

"Damn it, I told you the woman's going to be all right! Nobody notices that door in the Silver Rail and I locked all the upstairs doors and the one we just came out of. Anyhow, we won't be away from here much more than a half hour."

A frown grew on Ki's face. The voice was one he'd heard before, though he could not remember where.

"It's Ritter's territory," one of the others said. "He knows

123

it a lot better than we do, so let's quit worrying about the Starbuck woman and get on with our job."

Hearing Jessie's name had started alarm bells ringing in Ki's mind and the name Ritter had increased the ringing to a clamor. His memory brought back the struggle with the cartel gang in California whose leader was named Ritter, and he realized at once that the odds were overwhelming that the man who'd just ridden off and the California Ritter were one and the same.

Ki crept to the porch of the saloon and studied the feet of those inside. The clamor of the alarm bells stilled instantly as Ki's quick mind began working on a plan. Then, he realized that Jessie's feet, which should have been visible, were not among those he saw.

Carefully, a word at a time, Ki recalled what he'd heard Ritter say and then silently summarized his deductions. There are rooms above the saloon, his memory told him. There is a door at the side where the cartel men came out, but there is another door in the saloon that is not readily noticed. There are other locked doors upstairs, and behind one is where Jessie is being kept. And there is very little time left to find her.

A cowboy tune being whistled off-key and the grating of unsteady feet on the street behind him reached Ki's ears. Glancing over his shoulder, he saw a cowhand nearing the saloon in a reeling half-drunken stagger. He let himself relax into the sprawl of a drunk and the man stumbled past him without a glance.

Ki was on his feet in an instant, following the drunk into the saloon. He stepped aside as the eyes of those at the bar instinctively focused on the whistling newcomer, and he darted into the closest cover he saw, a dark niche. Pressing back into the shallow space, he felt a doorknob gouge into his thigh, and he realized at once that it must be the door

124

Ritter had mentioned. In an instant Ki opened the door and slipped through it.

Feeling his way up the stairway, he came to the first locked door. Knowledge that it would be locked had given Ki time to plan. He slid his *tanto* from its sheath and ignoring the damage he knew he would be doing to its sharp edge, he found the groove of the screw that held the doorknob in place and removed it, slanting the tip of the blade to use it as a screwdriver.

After sliding the doorknob off its square shaft, he took out the corner screws that held the plate in place, and now he could reach into the lock's inner mechanism. With his incredibly strong fingers, he grasped the end of the bolt and worked it out. The unlocked door swung open and Ki stepped silently into the dim hall.

As Jessie had done earlier, Ki tried each doorknob in turn, tapping gently, pressing an ear to the panel, but he heard no sound from the rooms beyond until he came to the last. Then, his cautious tapping brought response, a muffled thudding, a sound he could not recognize at once, but which common sense told him must be coming from Jessie.

Ki drew his *tanto* once more, and he used it as he just had. Grasping the doorknob in one hand, Ki pulled and the door budged. Hurriedly shoving the door to one side, Ki moved to its opening, and by the dim light that trickled into the room from the hallway saw Jessie, gagged and bound in a chair.

She was trying to twist her bonds in order to see the door, but the ropes that tied her to the chair had been drawn cruelly tight. Ki spoke at once.

"I'll have you out of here in a minute, Jessie," he said as he hurried to her side.

He placed the *tanto* to the rope that held her prisoner, but Jessie shook her head vigorously and raised her chin as

125

she moved her head. Ki interpreted the gesture with an understanding born of their long relationship and shifted his attention to her gag. Jessie sighed as he lifted away the rolled bandanna that had kept her silent for so long.

"I'm glad you understood, Ki," she said. "While I've been sitting here, I've worked out a plan."

"A plan for what?"

"For spoiling the cartel's scheme to take over Tombstone and turn it into their American headquarters! I heard enough after they caught me to figure out what they're trying."

"Are you sure about that, Jessie?" he asked.

"Do you remember a man named Ritter, Ki?"

"Yes, of course," Ki replied. "He led that cartel gang in California when—"

"Ritter's leading this one, too," Jessie broke in. "They talked about it even after they caught me. That means just one thing, and you know what it is."

"They intend to kill you, of course."

"Which I have no intention of letting them do. I knew you'd be here sooner or later."

"We can talk about that later," Ki said. "You said you had a plan. Tell me it, Jessie."

"I'm sure it'll work, but it depends on Ritter and his men finding me just the way they left me when they get back."

"Now, wait, Jessie!" Ki exclaimed, her words shaking his usual composure. "If you intend to let them take you with them, that's too dangerous even to think of!"

"Of course, it's dangerous," she agreed. "But these men are four of the cartel's top bosses in America, and two of the chief bosses in Europe will be getting here soon. Ki, if my plan works, we can cripple the cartel so badly that they won't be able to do anything important for the next ten years!"

Jessie's fervor was affecting Ki. He said, "Suppose you tell me what you're thinking about."

126

"Those four cartel bosses who captured me are big in America, but are small fry compared to the two who're on their way here from Europe. We've both heard their names. One's the mysterious one called the Count and the other is Schneider from Germany. Their coming here shows how important Tombstone is to their plans!"

Nodding slowly as he turned Jessie's words over in his mind, Ki said, "I can see how it would be. It's isolated, small, and in a place that's very rich in silver and copper and certainly there's bound to be some gold in the mountains around here."

"Exactly," Jessie said. "And it would be ideal for their headquarters for all those reasons. They've been planning this for a long time, Ki. I heard enough to convince me of that. And," she continued, "I'll bet anything that the cartel sent Bannon as a subterfuge. They figured that if we were very busy and completely preoccupied at the Circle Star, we'd have no time or wherewithal to consider any suspicious reports that might have come to us from the Arizona Territory."

"That makes sense to me. You think the two of us can stop them?"

Her first surge of excitement had subsided now and Jessie spoke very calmly. "I'm sure we can. Here's what we'll have to do. First, I'll have to let them take me to that secret base they set up in the mountains. I get the idea it's within ten or twelve miles from town. You'll be following when they move me, of course. Then, with you on the outside of their camp and me on the inside, we'll capture the bosses one at a time. When the two high-ranking cartel men get here, we won't have any trouble taking them. Without those leaders, the cartel can't do anything!"

"You make it sound very simple," Ki replied. "Aren't you underestimating this cartel crew, Jessie?"

Jessie's voice was as sober as Ki's when she replied. "I

might be. But I'm tired of being on the defensive, Ki! We've been letting them make the first move, and even if we've won a lot more than we've lost, it's time to teach them a lesson!"

Ki was silent for a moment; then he nodded and said quietly, "All right, Jessie. Let's try your plan. If we don't bring it off, I'll promise you it won't be for lack of trying!"

Chapter 12

"Here's my plan, Ki," Jessie said. "From what I heard Ritter telling the others, he wants to leave here late tonight to take me to that camp they have in the mountains."

"And I'll be following you," Ki said.

"Of course. It can't be very far. Ritter said he wanted to leave after midnight, so they could make the last part of the trip in daylight."

"That would put the place somewhere in the foothills of the mountains," Ki said. "Did he say how many men the cartel has here?"

"No. But you'll have plenty of time before we leave to get our rifles and my Colt from the hotel."

"And some extra *shuriken*," Ki said. "I can cut myself a *bo* someplace along the way. But I'd better get your Colt now and bring it to you before you leave."

"Where would I hide it in this skimpy outfit I've got on?"

"Yes, you're right. But at least take my *tanto*. I've got another at the hotel. I don't like you being in the hands of Ritter and his gang without a weapon."

"I've got one, Ki," Jessie said with a half smile. "I still have the little revolver Steve gave me. It's not like my Colt, but it doesn't show, tucked away where it is."

"You mean Ritter and his men didn't search you?" Ki asked incredulously.

"They were so staggered when they found me that they overlooked searching me. Besides, in this outfit I've got on, who'd think I would be carrying a pistol?"

"Suppose they decide to search you before you start for that hide-out?"

"It's a chance we'll have to take," Jessie replied. "But maybe I'd better take your *tanto* after all, Ki. They'll tie me up, of course, but I'm sure I can talk them into tying my wrists to the saddlehorn. That will give me a chance to get the *tanto* out and cut myself free."

"Remember what I showed you about flexing your muscles and tensing your wrist tendons when they start tying you. Then, they can't pull the ropes too tight," Ki said as he was freeing the *tanto* from his waistband.

"Don't worry. That's what I'm counting on," Jessie assured him. "Slip the *tanto* in my bodice, Ki. I don't think it'll show, and I can get to it by leaning forward."

As he slid the short, sheathed knife between Jessie's breasts he said, "They're not likely to notice it there. You'll be in the dark most of the time, anyway."

Jessie nodded, frowning abstractedly. After a moment the frown vanished and she told Ki, "I was worrying about the darkness, but now I realize that it's one of the things that's going to help us, Ki. I'll try to make my horse stumble now and then. The noise will keep you from losing us."

"I don't think we can plan much more, Jessie," Ki said. "All you can do is watch them closely and be ready to move at the right time. In that country, I can stay close enough to get to you in just a few seconds."

"Then we don't have anything more to worry about, do we?"

"Nothing except carrying out our plan," Ki replied. "It may not be the best one but it's as good as we can hope for with so little time. And speaking of time, I'd better get busy.

Ritter and his friends will be getting back any minute."

"Go on then," she said. "And stop worrying about me; I'll be all right."

After replacing her gag, Ki made quick work of fixing the door to the room and restoring the lock on the stairway door, using the tip of one of his *shuriken* as a screwdriver. In view of what Jessie had been able to tell him about the cartel's plans, he hoped he'd have time to make all the preparations that were needed.

He went down the stairs and stood in the dark nook at the end of the bar until he saw his chance to get out of the Silver Rail without attracting attention. Choosing Fremont Street because it had fewer saloons and stores to light it, Ki hurried to the back entrance of the OK Corral and had the liveryman saddle a horse.

Stopping at the Cosmopolitan Hotel, he put Jessie's pistol and holster into his saddlebags and added a handful of extra cartridges for her Colt. He dropped a sheath containing his reserve supply of *shuriken* in the saddlebags and clipped his spare *tanto* onto the waistband of his trousers. Jessie's rifle in its saddle sheath was leaning beside his own in a corner of the room, and he picked up both guns. As little as he liked guns, Ki was too experienced in fighting to give his adversaries an advantage.

Riding back to the Silver Rail, Ki did not risk turning into Sixth Street, but went on to the end of Fremont where Tombstone's graded streets became trails leading to open country. He circled off the end of Fremont and led his horse back toward Sixth, stopping in the rear of the parlor houses. After tethering the animal on one of the poles that supported a clothesline behind one of the houses, he walked to the position he'd held when watching the Silver Rail earlier in the evening and hunkered down to wait.

Minutes ticked away. A solitary man passed in front of

131

him and mounted the steps of the parlor house. Another man staggered out of the Silver Rail and meandered across to one of the doors, tapped, was greeted, and went in. A short time later a fight between two ladies of the evening broke out behind the parlor houses, and the silence was disturbed for several minutes by shrieks and curses before the fracas ended. A nickelodeon began tinkling in one of the parlor houses, its jarring notes subdued by walls and distance before they reached Ki's ears.

A wagon turned into Sixth. Ki paid little attention to it until it turned into the open space beyond the Silver Rail and creaked to a halt beside the building. He was watching the wagon with renewed interest when three riders came up the street, reined their mounts up beside the wagon, and dismounted. The man on the wagon dropped to the ground and joined the riders as they dismounted. Ki's interest took a sudden jump when the wagon driver opened a door at the front corner of the saloon and all four men disappeared inside.

On the upper floor of the Silver Rail, Jessie tensed momentarily when she heard the distant thudding of booted feet on the stairs, but by the time Ritter and his companions entered the room she'd regained control and was sitting in as relaxed a posture as she could manage within the bonds that held her to the chair. She stared straight ahead, as though her four captors did not exist.

"You better hold her head, Furnas," Ritter said. "She'll likely kick up a fuss."

Jessie felt a big hand clamp down on the top of her head while another hand closed over her eyes and nose. She fought down her instinctive reaction to protest and sat without struggling while Furnas pulled her head farther back.

Ritter said, "Blake, get that bandanna off her mouth.

132

And you better hang on, Furnas. She'll likely buck a lot when she gets a taste of this. I'll leave a message so Schneider and the Count will know where to meet us."

With her eyes covered, Jessie could only guess what was going on until the gag was whipped away and a hand grabbed her chin and pulled her mouth open. Then, the cold pressure of glass touched her lower lip and her mouth was suddenly filled with a bitter, acrid liquid.

To keep from choking, Jessie was forced to swallow when the liquid gushed into her mouth. She gulped, and as the bitter stuff ran down her throat, she recognized its taste. It was the knockout drops added to whiskey in saloons in order to quell troublemaking drunken patrons.

Feeling the bite of the liquid trickling down her throat brought an instinctive reaction. Jessie twisted her head and struggled against her bonds, but it was a short struggle. The chemical began its insidious work within a minute or two after she'd swallowed it. Her arms and legs grew lax and her struggles faded to stillness as consciousness left her.

Ki abandoned his crouch and dropped flat when the first of the four men came out of the Silver Rail. The cartel man went to the wagon and began fumbling along its bed. Ki stopped watching him when two others came out, carrying Jessie's limp form between them. At that moment he wanted nothing more than to rush across the street and liberate Jessie. He guessed at once that she'd been drugged. The sagging of her body as the men lifted her into the wagon confirmed his opinion.

Holding his instincts in firm control, Ki watched as the pair who'd carried Jessie out helped the third to draw a tarpaulin over the shallow bed of the vehicle and lash it in place. By then a fourth man was coming out the door. Ki had seen him before, in the encounter he and Jessie had with the cartel in California, and recognized him as Ritter.

Ki restrained his urgency to act until Ritter had climbed into the wagon seat and urged the horse ahead. Then, he dashed to the back of the parlor house where his horse was tethered and swung into the saddle. The wagon was already out of sight in the darkness, but during their quick conversation Jessie had given him the only clue he needed. The cartel's hideout was in the foothills of the mountains, and the only wagon road leaving Tombstone to the east started from Toughnut Street.

Ki turned his horse into Toughnut Street. There was no sign of the wagon and riders. He let the horse set its own pace until he saw the unfinished walls of the new courthouse blocking out the stars ahead and pulled into the concealment of the building's shadow. His wait was brief; he'd been there only a few minutes before the wagon and its three riders rumbled past. Ki waited until the creaking of the wagon and the thudding of their horses' hooves were almost inaudible; then he toed his own mount ahead and followed them.

Ki had no trouble following the wagon—even in the dense blackness of the night. The grating of iron wheels on the hard soil and hard rocks gave him all the guidance he needed.

Twice during the first hour or so he was in danger of getting too close to the wagon—when Ritter stopped to rest the horse at the top of long grades. Both times, Ki managed to rein in before the cartel men heard him, and as the night advanced, his ears grew attuned not only to the noise made by the wheels, but to the absence of noise when the wagon stopped moving.

As the miles fell behind the wagon and the land began to slope upward, progress became slower. Ki was forced to hold back his horse in order not to overtake the cartel group.

The upward slant grew still steeper, and as the horse pulling the wagon became wearier, Ritter was forced to rein in at shorter intervals to let the animal breathe. Ki, in turn, had to exercise even greater care, for in the still air even small sounds carried great distances.

Dawn's first pale streaks were beginning to outline the eastward horizon. After one of the wagon's frequent halts, Ki did not hear its wheels grating again after the usual amount of time. He waited a few minutes longer, straining his ears in the quiet, but no sound broke the stillness. After dismounting, Ki tethered his horse and started forward on foot.

He did not try to stay on the faint trail that the growing brightness revealed, but moved along its side. There was still cover in that arid sterile land. The only growth was a scattering of scrub cedars, stunted from lack of water, bent and twisted by the winds.

Occasionally the twin lines of the wagon's tracks vanished for thirty or forty yards where a rock outcrop surfaced. When this happened, Ki was forced to circle or zigzag until he came to a sandy spot or a patch of thin, crusted soil where the wheel marks and hoofprints showed again. He reached such a place, a shallow depression in the stony soil where the winds had whirled to create a long streak of loose gray sand, and he stopped abruptly when he saw no tracks in the soft stretch ahead.

Turning, Ki moved along the edge of the shallow stretch for a hundred yards or so, and when he still found no trace, he turned and retraced his steps to the point where he'd first come upon the sand deposit. He followed it down a gentle slope for another hundred yards. He stopped then and looked back, studied the terrain on both sides, and cut back at an angle toward his horse.

He'd covered half the distance between himself and the

animal before he found what he was seeking. The sign was not great, a spot no bigger than the palm of his hand where a chunk of the eroded softened rock showed a chalk-white gleam that stood out in sharp contrast to the gray, weathered surface of the big outcrop.

Ki walked quickly to the tell-tale mark, and a glance was enough to show him that the smooth parallel edges of the broken rut in the soft stone could only have been made by a wagon wheel. Hurrying now, Ki started back to the place where he'd left his horse.

Jessie's first impression as she stirred in slow return to awareness was one of total discomfort.

She was lying on her back when the effects of the knock-out drops began to wear off, and her first sensation was one of suffocation from the folds of the tarpaulin pressing on her face. Instinctively, she tried to raise her hands to push away the rough fabric, but her arms did not move. A second effort, this one a conscious command from her reviving brain, also failed.

Suddenly full consciousness returned to Jessie and she remembered everything that happened up to the point where the knockout drops had taken effect. Her last memory was of sitting bound in the chair, Furnas holding her head back while Ritter emptied the vial into her mouth. The harsh unpleasant taste of the liquid still clung to her tongue, and Jessie tried to swallow to rid herself of the pungently repulsive coating, but her throat and mouth were too dry.

She still did not quite know where she was, except that she was being jounced about uncomfortably, that her wrists and ankles were still bound, and that her back was sore. Twisting her wrists, Jessie felt the rough tarpaulin that covered her and recognized its texture.

She identified the jouncing, the grating of the wagon

wheels, the hoofbeats of the men riding alongside. Adding it all up, Jessie now knew that she was bound, lying in the bed of a wagon, covered by a tarpaulin, and that her scheme was working.

Belatedly remembering her weapons, Jessie squeezed her left arm to her side and felt the pressure of the little whore's gun in her armpit. She also felt the outline of Ki's *tanto* in the front of her dress. Knowing that the cartel gang had failed to search her lifted Jessie's spirits in spite of her discomfort. She relaxed and eased her position as much as possible while she set her mind to planning.

Mounted again and knowing which direction to take, Ki rode to the track he'd discovered. The sky was gray now, and along the jagged line of the eastern horizon the pink tinge of sunrise was beginning to appear. Reining his horse to a slow walk, Ki watched the rocky soil ahead for another sign that he was still on the route taken by the wagon.

He found what he was looking for before he'd covered another quarter mile. Ki saw the tracks of the wagon as well as the hoofprints of the horses accompanying the wagon.

A short distance ahead, the baked ground ahead of him suddenly vanished. Ki reined in and held his mount back while riding on. He came to a shoulder of rock. An upthrust stood beyond a narrow gap, which opened to reveal a quarter mile of open space. Holding his horse on a tight rein, Ki started for the little gap.

Lying in the wagon, half suffocated by the weight of the tarpaulin covering her face, Jessie managed to swing her head from side to side and twist her neck to get rid of the pressure of the rough stiff fabric. She'd just begun to breathe normally again when the wagon began to jounce, sway, and tilt. Jessie started to slide forward on its bed. Her feet hit some sort of obstacle she could not see, but her movement had disturbed the tarpaulin enough to take its pressure off her face permanently. She could breathe more easily now.

Suddenly, Jessie became aware that the sounds she'd heard during her first moments of returning consciousness had changed subtly. She could no longer hear the hoofbeats that had sounded beside the wagon, and a new noise was reaching her ears, the recurring screech of metal on metal. After she'd listened for a moment or two, she recognized the screech as the grating of the brake on the rear wheels and realized that the incline that had sent her sliding forward marked the beginning of a downgrade the wagon was now maneuvering.

A downgrade almost always meant a canyon in the rough mountain country over which she and Ki had ridden so recently. Jessie deduced that she'd been unconscious longer than she realized and that the wagon must be nearing the end of its journey.

She was not surprised when the wagon stopped swaying and thunking. The rasp of the brake stopped as did the grating of stone under the wheels. The vehicle rolled on quietly for a few minutes; then she heard Ritter's voice.

"All right," he called loudly, "we can ease up now. Get the Starbuck woman and we'll put her where she'll be safe. Then, we can have some breakfast."

Suddenly, the tarpaulin was dragged away. When daylight struck her eyes, Jessie squeezed her eyelids together. She heard unidentifiable noises while they were closed, and when she opened them, she saw Ritter's rough face just inches away.

"Well, you don't look like the drops hurt you much," he said. "And neither did getting here." When Jessie returned his stare, the cartel boss went on, "I hope you enjoyed the ride. It's the last trip you're ever going to take."

138

★

Chapter 13

For the first few hundred feet, the angle made by a cut-back in the narrow winding trail hid the canyon's floor from Ki. Then, he reached another sharp switchback and could look down again into the gaping opening. The wagon and three cartel men were just coming into sight from the side of the canyon where he stood watching.

Ki held his position for a moment. Knowing that if he could see them, they probably could see him, he toed the horse ahead. The next bend in the trail hid him from the eyes of the cartel gang. After dismounting, he wrapped the reins around a narrow stone that protruded from the wall and walked back to the bend.

By the time Ki reached a spot from which the canyon floor was once more visible, the wagon had come to a stop near a sort of shack that stood some distance from the walls of the canyon. Ki dropped to the ground and stretched out before glancing around the steep, jagged walls that encircled the big hole. It was a box canyon, its only entrance or exit the trail that had brought them to this point. Its walls were almost vertical, its floor concave, its eastern rim a jagged set of saw teeth against the brightening sky.

There was a small corral near the wall on Ki's right; three or four horses were penned in it. Beyond the corral the steep canyon wall was broken by a deep horizontal crease. The wall above the crease slanted upward in a low arch, forming a cut that extended back into the wall to form a sheltered area twenty or thirty feet wide. The growing light was not yet bright enough to illuminate the area, and as Ki watched, three men walked out of it and started toward the wagon.

Their appearance drew Ki's attention back to the wagon. The cartel men had dismounted by now and Ritter had gotten off the wagon. Two of the men were pulling away the tarpaulin that covered the wagon bed, and Ki saw Jessie as she sat up. Ritter had walked around to the tailgate and was talking to Jessie.

Unaware that Ki had reached the canyon and was watching, Jessie did not think to look up at the canyon walls. After Ritter finished his angry threat, he went on rather casually, "You might as well get down from the wagon. This is as far as we're going."

Jessie stood, a bit unsteady on her feet, still feeling the effects of the knockout drops.

Grasping the side of the wagon she stepped carefully to the ground. As she turned away from the wagon, Jessie swayed and felt herself about to fall. Ritter stepped forward, arms extended, but Jessie knocked them away.

"Don't touch me, Ritter," she snapped icily. She reached for the wagon and steadied herself. "Just looking at you and your friends makes my flesh creep."

"Go on and act high and mighty all you want to," Ritter said angrily. "You'll be begging us to let you die before we're through with you."

Jessie did not reply. She was pressing her left arm to her side, feeling the comforting pressure of the little pistol. Ritter stared angrily at her, then turned to the other cartel men.

"We'll put her in the shack till after we've rested. Then, we'll decide what to do next," Ritter said.

140

Before any of the cartel men could reply, the men whom Ki had seen reached the wagon. One of them hurried to Ritter and they held a brief, whispered conversation.

Ritter nodded and then said, "Take care of the horses and then make yourselves scarce for a while. We've got to talk about a few things that don't concern you."

Ignoring Jessie, Ritter went to join his companions. Two of the newcomers took charge of the saddle horses and the third grasped the bridle of the wagon horse, and they started leading the horses toward the corral.

Jessie stepped away hurriedly when the wagon moved, but the cartel group seemed uninterested in her at the moment. Leaving Jessie standing by herself, they were following Ritter to the door of the hut. Crowding together, they peered inside. Then, they stepped away from the little building and held a quiet conversation. Their talk lasted only a few moments, then they returned to where Jessie stood.

She was swaying a bit now, and when Ritter motioned toward the shack, she began walking slowly and unsteadily toward the hut. One of the cartel men took a step toward her, but stopped when Jessie motioned him away. She went into the hut and was followed by Ritter.

For a moment Jessie could make out no details in the dark, little structure. As her eyes grew accustomed to the semidarkness, she saw that there were two beds in the hut, each against a wall. One of the beds was unoccupied, but in the other a man lay stretched out, his face to the wall. His right arm was extended above his head. There was a manacle on his right wrist, the short chain from the iron band attached by a heavy bolt in the bedframe.

"Lie down on the bed," Ritter commanded. "Stick your arm up."

As she moved closer to the empty bed, Jessie saw that it also had a manacle bolted to one of its frames. She did not argue. She laid down and without waiting for Ritter's command extended her right arm to the headboard. With a grunt, Ritter bent over and closed the cuff around Jessie's wrist. Then, he snapped the lock shut. Stepping back, he looked at the two prisoners for a moment, then turned, and left the shack.

Stretched flat beside the trail above the canyon, Ki saw Ritter come out of the shack alone and make a remark to the other three cartel men. The group started walking toward an overhang, entered the dark area below it, and disappeared.

Ki frowned thoughtfully as he walked back to his horse. He did not mount, but led the animal slowly along the zigzagging, downsloping trail. His eyes searched the canyon wall for a place to camp.

More than halfway to the bottom, he found what he'd been looking for, a vertical cut wide enough to let the horse enter easily and deep enough to accommodate both him and the horse. He tethered the animal to a boulder and hunkered down beside the big stone, his mind busy recalling what he'd seen.

Logic told him that the canyon was the cartel gang's hide-out, and that having reached it, they would stay there at least for a short while. They'd need sleep and their horses would have to be rested before starting back to Tombstone. Suddenly, Ki realized that he must be as tired as Ritter's crew. He lifted his saddlebags and the rifles off the horse and took them a step or two back into the slit, laid his saddlebags on top of the weapons, then unrolled his blanket, stretched out, and went to sleep.

For the first few minutes after Ritter left the hut, Jessie stayed motionless, her face to the wall, thinking over her situation. She could see no immediate solution to her hazardous position, but was confident that Ki would rescue her. Together, they would work out a plan that would stop the cartel group from carrying out any plans of their own.

Clumsily, she turned over. The manacled man on the other bed was watching her, but she ignored him while she wriggled and twisted until she found a position that did not contort her body or put a strain on her right arm. Then, she looked at her fellow prisoner and said, "Since we're both in the same situation, I suppose introductions are in order."

"I was thinking the same thing," he replied. "My name's Terrance Ryan, ma'am."

Jessie hesitated for a moment, decided no purpose would be served by trying to conceal her identity, and replied, "I'm Jessica Starbuck."

"Starbuck?" Ryan said quizzically. "You wouldn't be related to the late Mr. Alex Starbuck, would you?"

A flag of caution waved in Jessie's mind. "Why?" she countered. "Did you know him?"

"No, ma'am. But my chief did. I've heard him say quite a few times that this country lost one of its finest men when Mr. Starbuck got killed a few years back."

"Who is your chief?" Jessie asked, still cautious.

"I'm on Governor Fremont's staff, ma'am. I guess you've heard of him?"

"Of course, I have. He's a very famous man. Exactly what do you do for him?"

"Well, I went to work for him when he was building that southern railroad line, and when it failed, I stayed with him to be his secretary and jack-of-all-trades. I just do whatever he tells me to."

"Governor Fremont sent you here?"

"Not exactly here," the young man said. He frowned, but it somehow became an Irish smile. "He sent me to

143

Tombstone, but here's where I ended up."

"So it seems," Jessie replied. She smiled in spite of her predicament, and then asked, "I'm interested in knowing why, if you don't mind telling me."

This time the young officer hesitated. At last he said, "Seeing who you are, Miss Starbuck, and that you're in the same fix I am, I don't suppose it'd hurt to tell you. I guess you know Sheriff Behan?"

"I've met him," Jessie nodded.

"Well, before Fremont was appointed governor, the sheriff was after the job Fremont got."

"Sheriff Behan wanted to be governor?"

Ryan nodded and then went on. "I guess you can figure out that the sheriff and Fremont wouldn't be real close friends. Of course, the governor gets a lot of news from different people; it seems he's got friends just about everywhere. He got a hint from one of them that somebody was going to stir up a lot of trouble in Tombstone. He wondered if Sheriff Behan might be behind it, so he sent me to find out."

Jessie was silent for several moments. Behan hadn't impressed her as being the type to get involved with the cartel, but she'd held that opinion of a few other men—only to find she'd misjudged them.

She asked Ryan, "Are you saying that the sheriff is responsible for your being held prisoner here?"

"Oh, no, Miss Starbuck! That man Ritter, the one who brought you in here, he hasn't got any more use for the sheriff than he has for Governor Fremont. I've heard him talk about both of them, and I'm sure that they're not in cahoots."

"How long have you been here?"

"Close to two weeks."

"How did the—" Jessie stopped suddenly when she realized what she was about to ask and changed her question. "Was Ritter the one who brought you here?"

"He sure was!" Ryan exclaimed angrily. "But I acted the fool, or I wouldn't be here at all!"

"Maybe you'd better explain," Jessie suggested.

Ryan hesitated, but then he went on, "Well, I've said so much already that I guess I'd better finish. Like I told you, you wouldn't be here unless we're both on the same side."

"I'm not sure yet which side you're on," Jessie told him bluntly. "Everything you've said so far seems to hold together, but I'm still not quite convinced."

"I'm not real proud of telling you how I got put here, Miss Starbuck," Ryan said, an angry frown sweeping over his face. "But I guess everybody plays the fool at one time or another."

"Suppose you go ahead and tell me," Jessie suggested. "It might clear up any questions I have."

"Somebody left me a note at the hotel where I was staying," he said. "It wasn't signed or anything, but whoever wrote it said he had some information I could use and told me he'd meet me at the Silver Rail Saloon. I went there and while I was waiting, I ordered a drink. That's the last thing I knew until I woke up in this place, handcuffed to this cot."

"By now I'm sure you've figured out who wrote that note," Jessie said dryly.

"It couldn't have been anybody but Ritter," Ryan told her, anger creeping into his voice. "Maybe he didn't sit down and write it, but he sure had it sent."

"How can you be sure of that?" Jessie inquired.

"Because after I'd come to, he came in and started asking questions about Fremont."

Jessie was sure that she recognized the ring of truth in Ryan's story, but even this was not enough to persuade her

145

that he was what he claimed to be. She decided that before confiding in the personable young man, it would be wise for her to do a bit of testing.

"I'm sure you didn't answer those questions," she said, "or did you?"

"I sure didn't. I knew by then I was in trouble."

"Did he ask about the governor's family life?"

"No, ma'am. He didn't say a word about Mrs—" Ryan broke off and shook his head. Then, he said, "It didn't occur to me till right this minute, but you and Mrs. Fremont have the same first name. Hers is Jessie, too."

"Yes, I know," Jessie said. "I wondered if you'd remember that."

"You don't believe what I've told you, do you, Miss Starbuck?" Ryan asked. "Maybe you think I'm just trying to worm something out of you to pass on to Ritter."

"That had occurred to me."

"Well, I'm not! The only thing I want to do to Ritter is knock his head off!"

By now, Jessie was convinced. "I think we'll both be free before very long," she said. "I have someone trailing me and soon he'll come in and release me."

"That sounds like you expected to be put in here," Ryan said. "It gives me an idea you've dealt with Ritter before."

"Yes—and with some of the people he works for. You see, my father left me property, and there are a number of people trying to get their hands on it."

"If there's any way I can help you, Miss Starbuck, I'm sure the governor would want me to," Ryan offered.

"We'd be fools if we didn't work together, Mr. Ryan," Jessie said. "There are only the three of us, and Ritter has several men."

Ryan said, "And they've got guns and we haven't."

"We will have, when Ki gets here," Jessie assured him.

146

"Ki? That sounds like he's Chinese."

"Ki is half Japanese and half American," Jessie said. "He was my father's righthand man, and he's now my good friend and helper."

"Do you have any idea when he's going to be here?"

Jessie shook her head. "Only that he'll get here sometime after dark. Now, I don't know about you, Mr. Ryan, but I'm a little bit tired. I'm going to try to sleep, and I suggest you do the same."

"My friends call me Terry, Miss Starbuck."

"And I'm Jessie to mine," she replied. "Now, let's rest. We're going to have a busy night and we need to be fresh."

Ki slept lightly, as he always did. The sound of horses' hooves thunking on the hard ground of the trail outside his improvised hideaway roused him. Noting that the sun was now high in the sky, he moved quietly to the mouth of the little slit and dropped flat as the hoofbeats grew louder. The riders were still hidden behind the massive rock outcrop, which created a curve in the trail. Soon, though, Ki could hear the conversation of the riders.

"It is not good organization, I tell you, Count!" one of them was saying in a pronounced Teutonic accent. "We have made a long journey for this meeting. Why didn't Ritter stay to meet us himself?"

"Ritter is taking care of an emergency," the other man replied. His voice was light, and he spoke with the cultivated intonation of one to whom English was a second language, but learned at an upper-class British school or from a tutor. "I suggest that we do not mention our inconvenience, Schneider."

"Always underlings must be in their place kept," Schneider said. "But you are perhaps right. I will say nothing."

Ki watched the two as they came in complete view from

147

around the shoulder that had hidden them. Both men wore well-tailored business suits, and both of them sat their mounts in European fashion.

Schneider gave the appearance of being grossly fat, though he was only a bulky man with a red face, perspiring freely in the warm sunshine. Under his square jaw he had a wattle of fat that hung over his high collar. His small blue eyes were almost lost in his puffy eyelids and were overshadowed by his bushy blond eyebrows.

His companion, the Count, was slender, and his hands were almost dainty on the reins. The color of the skin drawn tautly over his high cheekbones was so pink that Ki thought at first he wore rouge. His suit was black, matching his short beard and thin waxed mustache.

"That is good of you to say nothing," the Count said as they passed by Ki in his hiding place. "We must let Ritter believe he will be in full charge of our operations in America until the time comes to get rid of him."

"I promise you, *mein freund,* he will get no hints from me," Schneider replied as they rode on out of earshot.

Ki waited until he could no longer hear the hoofbeats of their horses before getting up and returning to his blankets. His face was expressionless, but he was worried. He thought of the increased odds that he now faced in his mission to free Jessie from the cartel's clutches.

Chapter 14

Ki did not at all like what he'd heard. Being well acquainted with the cartel's merciless methods, he was positive that Schneider and the Count would demand that Ritter use the most ruthless methods possible on Jessie. He was tired from his sleepless night, but he gave up any thought of rest. Knowing also that he must not risk diminishing his energy, he ate a few bites of hardtack and jerky, threw his saddlebags over his shoulder, and started down the trail that led to the floor of the canyon.

Moving at a slow trot, Ki reached the last curve in the trail before the final short stretch that ended on the canyon floor. He was standing almost directly above the corral and, looking down, saw the animals that Schneider and the Count had ridden among the other half dozen horses in the enclosure. There was no one moving on the canyon floor, from which Ki deduced that the European bosses must have called their American cohorts together for a conference.

Dropping flat on his belly, Ki discovered that he could see far enough into the horizontal crevasse the gang used as a shelter to observe the group of men gathered around the Count and Schneider. He saw Ritter also and he recognized one of the men who'd ridden beside the wagon that carried Jessie to the hide-out.

There were others in the shadows whom he could not place, but he assumed they were guards who had been stationed at the canyon. Ritter was talking and now and then Schneider or the Count would nod or shake his head or put in a word or two. The group was sitting on blankets that had been spread to cushion them from the cold, hard stone of the ledge, which hinted that their discussion would be a long one. Ki decided at once to try to get close enough to hear what was being said.

Studying the steep wall beyond the corral, Ki could now see cracks and tiny crevasses in the sheer expanse of rock above the lip that formed an overhang. He reached a decision. Pushing his saddlebags into a narrow opening between two massive boulders, he started following the rim of the canyon toward the lip. As he picked his way over the contours, Ki began flexing his fingers.

When he could look down the sheer rock wall that dropped away below him and see the bulge of the overhang, Ki stopped and lay flat on the edge. He studied the drop below. At close range, he could see plainly that although the wall was sheer, it was even less solid than it appeared from a distance.

Here and there inch-wide cracks broke the face, and there were places where thin slabs had broken away and left narrow miniature ledges. Swinging his legs out and over the sheer drop of almost a hundred feet, Ki used his toes to feel for the first ledge. It was no more than an inch wide and was just beyond reach of his toes. He locked his fingers into a crack and lowered himself to dangle against the wall.

For half the distance down, Ki had easy going. The cracks were plentiful and spaced closely enough together to make his descent almost as simple as walking down a flight of stairs. Then, the cracked area began to merge with the less broken part. Progress became more difficult and suddenly Ki found himself without a convenient array of cracks or protrusions to provide grips and footholds.

150

Peering from one side to the other, Ki saw a small knob near his waist that offered a precarious fingerhold. Locking his hand into a claw, he grasped the tiny knoblike projection and let himself drop, toes pointing downward. He felt the shock as his stiffened toes landed on the narrow projection, and he clung to the knob while he searched for a support that would stabilize his precarious position.

He finally found one, a crack in the wall below and to the left, with a knobby hump close enough to it to give him a handhold to cling to while reaching for the crack. Squeezing his right hand between the cliff and his body, Ki managed to reach the knob. He caught it with his right hand and swung free, stretching his left arm to reach the crack. He scraped for a handhold as his clutching fingers entered the crack, and he got them locked inside the miniature hole an instant before his movement pulled his left hand away from the knob.

With his new hold secured, Ki was now almost squatting, his knees spread wide apart, the toes of his right foot beginning to become cramped. The slant of the overhang was now less than two or three yards below him, and between his toes and the lip there was an area perhaps a foot square where chunks of stone had split away from the wall, forming a shelf perhaps six inches wide and almost a yard long.

Thin, shallow vertical cracks ran upward from the shelf, but he could not see whether or not they were wide enough to allow him to thrust his fingers into them or deep enough for him to close his hand in order to use them as a secure support. As he clung and debated his chances, Ki suddenly realized that he could hear the voices of the cartel gang now, but they were whispers he was unable to understand.

Realizing that his next move would take him to a point where he could hear clearly, Ki took the risk offered by the split. Extending his arm as far as possible, he launched himself with the tips of his toes toward the cracked area. His outstretched hand scraped the edges of the depression that was his target, and his sudden move almost dislodged his toes from their precarious perch. Ki felt himself about to fall.

With supreme effort, he brought his body erect, putting his clawing fingers above the bottom edge of the depression just before his toes were pulled off their dangerous perch. His fingertips caught the ledge, but he had not secured a firm grip before he felt himself beginning to drop.

Only Ki's catlike quickness and his steel fingertips saved him from plummeting down the sheer granite wall and rolling off the slanting lip. Sweeping his extended hand upward, Ki renewed his grasp on the cracks. With a firm hold to support and stabilize him, he could now shove his toes forward and lock them over the shallow ledge. He knew his support was only momentary, and he twisted in a partial turn that made his temporary toehold even more precarious, but his desperate move succeeded.

Before his weight dragged his toes off the ledge, Ki thrust his hand deeper into the crack and got a firm grip. After that, it was easy for him to regain his toehold, and to secure himself still further, he slipped his other hand into a narrow fissure that had been invisible while he'd been in his former position. He found a projection that he could grasp.

While he was twisting and swaying in the air above the lip, the voices of the cartel men had become more audible, and when Ki at last secured himself and braced his muscles, he could hear them quite clearly.

"We have no choice but to wait," Schneider was saying. "We must get rid of the Starbuck woman and her helper."

"Well, we've got the woman," Ritter said. "We can get rid of her when you say the word."

"Do not be in a hurry, Ritter," the Count said in his

precise manner. "Jessie Starbuck will serve us doubly, now that we hold her. She will lure the Oriental to us, and when we have them both, it will be easy to make them talk."

"I wouldn't be too sure," one of the men said. "She was tightlipped when we tried to get anything out of her back in town."

Ki did not recognize the man's voice, but from what he'd said realized that he was one of the trio who'd been with Ritter at the Silver Rail.

"I will guarantee to make her talk," the Count said confidently. "My methods do not fail."

"You haven't run up against anybody like that Starbuck dame, Count," Greener said. "She's got ice water in her veins instead of blood."

"Maybe the men will feel better if you tell 'em what you got in mind, Count," Ritter suggested.

"Of course," the Count agreed. "There are how many of you here—eight?—and all of you seem strong and lusty. We will strip the Starbuck woman and lash her spread-eagle to stakes and you will then take turns raping her."

When the Count finished, there was silence among the cartel leaders. Then, Furnas broke the hush to say, "That don't appeal to me, Count. There's—"

"I did not ask your approval, Furnas," the Count broke in, his voice slicing the air as a knife would cut warm butter. "You will do as you are commanded, now or in the future. We do not allow anyone to question our commands. Is that clear?"

"It's clear, but I still have my doubts," Furnas insisted. "And this Starbuck woman ain't like most. She's got more guts than a lot of men I've seen."

"You lack experience," the Count said. "I have seen only two women who did not respond to my method. Even those two gave up their secrets when I used certain instruments

153

I have on the vulnerable parts of their bodies. No, you need not worry. The Starbuck woman will tell us what we must know to take over the properties Alex Starbuck left to her. Now, I have had enough of this discussion. The matter is settled!"

A silence fell on the group after the Count stopped speaking. Ki's anger was surging over him in waves, for the Count's remarks had burst through his stoicism. He felt the urge to drop at once to the ground and eliminate the sadistic monster. He smothered his emotions and listened when Schneider began speaking.

"The Count is right," he said. "We must have the Starbuck riches, and there is no place in our organization for those who do not obey orders. Now, I suggest that we end this meeting. The Count and I have had a long trip. We are not used to riding long distances on horseback. There are certain other matters to discuss, but we will do that later."

Ki had not anticipated Schneider's suggestion. As the voices of the men below faded into unintelligible, garbled conversations, he started scrambling toward the top of the cliff. Climbing up was much easier than descending. Ki got to the top before any of the cartel's men had left the ledge, and he moved quickly away from the rim before anyone glimpsed him. After hurrying back to the boulders where he'd hidden his saddlebags, he retrieved them and rushed back to the hidden vale where his horse and other gear were concealed.

As soon as the sun had fallen low enough to cast the shadow of its western rim on the canyon's floor, Ki wrapped a *surushin* around his waist under his loose-fitting jacket and tucked a black *ninja* mask into one of its capacious pockets. He took a spare sheath filled with *shuriken* from his saddlebags. After a quick examination of the star-shaped throw-

154

ing blades, he strapped the second sheath on his right forearm to match the one already in place on his left.

Looking at the rifles leaning against his saddle, Ki shook his head, deciding quickly that they would be more of an encumbrance than a help in carrying out his half-formulated plan. He dug Jessie's Colt out of his saddlebags, however, and stuck it in the waistband of his baggy trousers. Then he dropped a box of shells in his jacket pocket. Preparation for his mission had taken less than five minutes. Ki left the cleft and started down the rocky trail to the canyon floor.

At that hour the trail was partly shadowed. When he reached the first twist in the trail's writhing curves, he looked at the canyon floor. Ki nodded with satisfaction when he saw that the shadowline had almost reached the shack where he'd seen Ritter take Jessie earlier in the day.

Looking toward the ledge, Ki saw that the cleft beneath it was in an even deeper shadow than the canyon floor. By closing his eyes briefly from time to time to keep his irises enlarged, Ki made out the forms of several men grouped in a rough circle beneath the overhang.

Under the overhanging lip, the shadows were too deep and the distance too great for Ki to identify faces, but because they were standing around chatting idly he could tell that the meeting that Schneider had ended so abruptly had not yet been resumed.

Nothing could have fitted his own purpose better, Ki thought, as he peered along the curving stretch of canyon wall that lay between him and the overhanging ledge. His sharp eyes found what he'd been hoping for less than fifty yards from where he was standing: a fissure deep enough to hide him as he made his way down to the canyon floor.

Picking his way carefully along the trail until he was out of sight of the cartel's men, Ki reached the cleft. Donning his *ninja* mask, which covered his head except for a narrow eye-slit, he began his descent. Bracing his back on one side of the fissure, pushing with hands and feet against its opposite side, Ki worked his way down to the bottom and stepped out on the canyon floor.

By now the sun had dropped lower, and the hut itself was in deep shadow. Calling on all the skill he'd learned from the masters under whom he'd studied, Ki began working his way to the shack. Crawling no faster than a lazy snail, he took a zigzag course to make the most of every depression in the broken ground. When he lifted his head to survey his surroundings, his midnight-black attire blended with the deep duskiness of the canyons' back wall.

By the time Ki's slow progress brought him to the shack, the narrowing strip of sunlight on the floor had touched the back wall of the canyon and was beginning to move up it. Ki was just getting ready to stand up and make a final dash when he heard muffled footsteps and swiveled his head to see a man approaching from the overhang. There was no time left for him to get inside the hut. Ki brought his outstretched legs together, pulled his arms to his sides and lay motionless.

Whistling tunelessly, the man entered the shack. From the corner of his eyes, Ki saw that the newcomer was carrying a plate in each hand.

As the man entered the hut, Ki heard him say, *"Tengo sus cenas."*

Ki was expecting Jessie's voice to reply, but it was a man who answered, *"No tenemos hambre al momento. Comeremos más adelante."*

"Cualquier que quieres." There was a shrug in the man's voice. In a moment he ambled out and started walking back toward the overhang.

Ki gave him a moment and then slipped into the hut. He removed his hood. His eyes were adjusted to darkness, but

156

not to the blackness that veiled the interior of the small building. He stopped just inside the door as Jessie greeted him.

"Ki! You got here earlier than I expected!"

"I had to wait until the canyon floor was dark, Jessie," Ki told her. His pupils had dilated by now, and as his vision cleared he saw Jessie, lying on a narrow bed at one side of the room, and he could identify the other occupant as a man.

Jessie said quickly, "This is Terrance Ryan, Ki. He's an aide to Governor Fremont. It seems that the—that our friends have made him their prisoner, too." Without more than a token pause, she went on, "I told you Ki would be here as soon as it was dark enough, Terry."

"If I say I'm glad to see you, Ki, it would be understating my feelings. Until Jessie told me you were coming to help us, I was about to give up."

"Why are you being held?" Ki asked.

"Damned if—excuse me, Jessie—if I know. But I've been here long enough to know I don't want to stay."

Jessie broke in. "Ki, before we start talking about why Terry's here and why I'm chained out here and all the rest of it, will you see what you can do about getting us free? This shackle on my wrist is awfully uncomfortable, and I know Terry's must be even worse because he's been in here for several days."

"It's too dark to see how those shackles are fastened," Ki replied, "but let me feel them and see what I can do."

He dropped to one knee beside the head of Jessie's narrow bed and for a moment fingered the iron band that circled her wrist and the padlock. Then, he ran his fingertips down the chain and over the eyebolt that attached it to the heavy timber which formed one end of the bed.

"Well?" Jessie asked as Ki got to his feet.

"I can't pick the padlock because I don't have any kind of tool with me," Ki said. "But I think I can take out the bolt that holds them to the bed. It might be better to do that instead of opening the shackle because you can remove the bolts yourselves if you need to, even if I'm not here."

"If you're not—" Jessie began, her voice showing her surprise. "I thought you came to get us out of here!"

"That was my plan," Ki said, "but I didn't know you had company."

"Terry was here first," Jessie said. "I'm the company. But get us loose if you can before we start discussing plans."

Ki dropped to his knees beside the bedpost and clamped his muscular fingers on the eye of the bolt. With his other hand's fingertips, he found a slight hold on the nut at the bolt's opposite end. Applying all the pressure he could muster, he twisted his hands in opposing directions, and after a short struggle, he felt the bolt begin to turn. After that, it was easy for him to remove it.

Handing the eyebolt to Jessie, Ki said, "Walk around and get your muscles loosened up, Jessie. Now that I know how to take the bolts out, I'll have the other one out right away."

Moving carefully in the semidarkness of the hut, Jessie began pacing, three steps forward, three steps back. While Ki was working on Ryan's manacle, she started bringing Ki up to date on their situation.

"Governor Fremont sent Terry here to check up on Sheriff Behan, Ki," she began. "Somehow, the governor got word that there might be some trouble in Tombstone. Since the sheriff is one of his political opponents, Governor Fremont got the idea that he might be responsible for starting it."

"And you've told him—" Ki began.

Jessie cut in quickly. "Nothing. We haven't talked a lot, but Terry's ready to help us if we need him."

"We'll need him," Ki said, trying but not succeeding in keeping worry from creeping into his voice. "We'll need every bit of help we can get, Jessie. There are more of them across the canyon now, and that makes the odds greater against us."

"We've faced heavy odds before, Ki," Jessie reminded him.

"Yes. But this time we're not facing the second echelon of command. We've got the top bosses here, and they have some very nasty plans for you. We've got to keep Schneider and the Count from getting their hands on you!"

Chapter 15

When Jessie heard the names Ki mentioned, her face grew as sober as his. She said, "We miscalculated, Ki. We should have arranged for support from the law."

"You're right, of course," he replied. "But Schneider and the Count are here, and it's impossible to overlook them." Ki had freed Ryan's arm now. He handed him the eyebolt.

Ryan said, "Thanks, Ki. I don't suppose you mind me calling you Ki, even if we haven't been formally introduced."

One of Ki's rare smiles formed on his face. He replied, "Ki will have to do, Terry. It's all the name I have." Turning to Jessie, he said, "I suggest that we tell our new friend what the situation is."

"Please do, Jessie!" Ryan urged. "You and Ki have been talking in riddles so far."

"We had good reason for that, Terry," Jessie said.

Ryan frowned as he went on, "I got the idea when we were talking earlier that you wanted to say more. If you were holding back, I'd like to know why."

"I wasn't being secretive without a good reason, Terry," Jessie protested. "And I'm afraid that I won't be able to be complete."

"Tell me as much as you can, then," he suggested. "Maybe I can guess at some of the things you don't want to talk about."

"Well," Jessie began a bit slowly, trying to think of what

161

she should and shouldn't say, "there's a group of European industrialists trying to expand into this country." She paused, groping for words, not yet ready to mention the totally ruthless nature of the cartel.

Ryan said, "European firms set up branches in this country all the time, Jessie. Why should this bunch bother you?"

"Because these men are ruthless in a way that most businessmen aren't," she answered soberly. "They tried to get Alex to join them, but he refused. Then when he—died, they began attacking me. I suppose they thought that because I'm a woman I'd be afraid to fight back." Jessie paused again, but could find no way to explain quickly. She finally compromised by saying, "I think they're trying to set up some kind of headquarters in the Arizona Territory. That's what Ki and I came here to find out."

"Have you found that out?" Ryan asked.

"I think you know the answer," Ki added before Jessie could reply. "They took Jessie prisoner because they have an idea they can use force to make her transfer the Starbuck industries to them. Is that enough of an answer?"

"It'll satisfy my curiosity until we have a better time to talk," Ryan said. "I'm sure the rumor that reached Governor Fremont was a version of what's going on. And I don't believe Sheriff Behan is involved in it in any way."

"You're right, I'm sure," Jessie replied.

"How many of them are here?" Terry asked. "I've only seen a few since I've been here, but I've heard enough strange voices talking outside to know there must be more."

"Ten, at least," Ki told him. "But I don't expect the Count and Schneider to expose themselves to danger. They're the generals; they stay out of the line of fire and give orders."

"That still makes at least eight," Jessie commented.

"Jessie," Ki broke in, "we've got plans to make and very little time to make them."

162

"How can we make plans until we know what they're up to?" Jessie asked.

"We can't, of course," Ki replied. "So far, none of them knows I'm in the canyon. But we've got to act tonight."

"Of course, we must," Jessie said. "What can we do tonight, though? You have your own weapons, but they're not of much use to me or Terry. All I've got is that little gun."

"You mean you have a gun, Jessie?" Terry asked. "Why didn't you tell me before? We might have had a chance—"

Jessie interrupted him to say, "There wasn't any reason to. And it's not much use unless you're close to your target."

Ki took out Jessie's Colt. "I did manage to bring you this, Jessie. I had to climb down a cliff to get here, so I couldn't bring the rifles, but they're hidden up on the canyon rim."

"Give the Colt to Terry," Jessie said. "He's got pockets in his clothes."

As Ki passed the revolver to Terry, he said, "We've got to make a plan of some kind, even if all it does is keep us from doing the wrong thing at the wrong time."

"What do you suggest?" she asked.

"All I'm suggesting now is that we've got to get you out of here at once—before the Count and Schneider get their own plans working. From what I overheard earlier, they have very definite plans for you."

As Ki finished speaking, he stepped to the door and glanced toward the end of the canyon. The dying fire on the ledge had been rekindled and now its flames danced brightly. He could see the figures of the cartel gang silhouetted against the glow that spread across the overhanging lip.

"Are they doing anything?" Jessie asked.

"No. But they could start moving any minute." Ki paused and went on, "It's more than likely they're planning what to do when daylight comes." Turning back to Jessie and Terry, he said, "Let's put off making a plan or moving for a few minutes. I can get close enough now to hear what they're saying. You two stay here. I'll be back very soon."

As Ki started toward the fire, he pulled his ninja hood back over his face. With the darkness to conceal him, there was no need for too stealthy an approach. As soon as the hood was in place, Ki began trotting. He'd covered more than half the distance to the ledge before he realized that the faster pace was a mistake. His foot struck a small boulder. The misstep not only broke Ki's steady stride, but the boulder's movement grated like coarse sandpaper on the baked earth. The sound brought an instant challenge.

"Quién pasa?" a voice called from the darkness only a few yards ahead.

Ki dropped flat. He heard feet scuffling ahead, and against the glow from the fire he saw the silhouetted figure of a man rising to his feet, rifle in hand. For a moment the sentry whom Ki hadn't anticipated stood peering from side to side, trying to locate the source of the sound. Ki remained prone, hoping the man would hold his position, but the sentry began walking slowly toward him.

Ki froze when he realized that unless the other man changed course it was inevitable that he would be discovered. The man was close enough to him now to hear even Ki's quiet movements. When he saw that an evasive movement was no longer possible, Ki gave up the idea of doubling back. The sentry kept advancing slowly, his rifle held across his body now, the firelight outlining his figure and glinting on the rifle barrel.

When the man was so close that with his next step he'd plant his foot on Ki's body, Ki leaped up. He grasped the rifle barrel with one hand and brought his free arm around in a strike.

Ki's blow was quick. The sharp point of his elbow smashed into the fragile bones of the sentry's temple and sent sharp slivered points driving into his brain. The man had no time to shout. Although the stabbing shards killed the sentry instantly, the muscles of his arms tightened in a death throe. His forefinger closed on the trigger of his rifle as he sagged. The rifle barked, and the flash from its muzzle brightened the night. Then, the echoes of the shot began reverberating from the canyon's rocky walls.

Ki held on to the rifle as the man crumpled to the ground. Before the echoes of the shot had died away, he was heading back to the shack at a run. He saw Jessie and Terry Ryan standing outside and, without stopping to explain, pushed them back into the shack.

"What happened, Ki?" Jessie asked.

"I've stirred things up," he said. "It'll take them a few minutes to start looking for us, but we don't have much time to waste."

"They shot at you?" Terry asked.

"No. I ran into a sentry. He had his finger on the trigger and closed his hand when he died," Ki explained.

"You killed him, then?" Jessie asked, her voice a controlled whisper.

"Of course," Ki replied, handing Jessie the rifle. "Keep this, Jessie. We'll need it."

"But, Ki—" Jessie began.

Ki broke in, "That shot's changed things for us, Jessie. This place will be alive with enemies in a few minutes. We've got to make some plans—quickly."

"We can attack them now while they're still disorganized," Terry suggested.

"No, Terry," Jessie replied. "Ki has the same idea that's

165

occurred to me. Even in the dark and with this extra gun, we'd be fools to do that. Fighting at night wastes ammunition, and we don't have enough to spare. We might start a fight we couldn't win."

"Jessie hasn't mentioned the most important thing," Ki added. "We've got to get her out of reach of that gang. She's the one they're after. We've got to try to leave as quickly as possible."

"Run away?" Terry asked. Though his face was hidden in the darkness, a frown showed in the tone of his voice.

"Ki doesn't intend for us to start back to Tombstone, I'm sure," Jessie put in quickly. "And neither do I."

"Of course not," Ki agreed. "There are two more rifles and a good supply of ammunition up on the canyon rim. Once we get up there and get our hands on them, we've got a chance to win."

"Let's stop wasting time now and start moving," Jessie said. "You know the way, Ki. We'll follow you."

Ki turned, but the step he started was never finished. The fire on the ledge was no longer glowing, and the canyon was veiled in darkness. He turned back to the others.

"Move carefully," he cautioned. "They've put out their fire. That means they're probably moving in on us right now. We haven't any time. Let's get started."

"Stay close to Ki, Terry," Jessie told Ryan. "And don't use your gun unless you can see what you're shooting at. I'll be right behind you with the rifle."

Moving at a fast walk, Ki led Jessie and Terry at right angles to the shack, heading directly for the canyon wall. They walked in silence. From time to time Ki flicked his eyes upward to orient himself by the canyon wall. When the level canyon floor began to slope upward, he turned and headed for the trail that led out of the canyon.

The darkness was abysmal even to their night-conditioned eyes. Big chunks of granite that had fallen to the floor tripped their feet as they advanced, and more than once they bumped into chunks of stone half the size of a house and had to detour around them.

Time was meaningless now. At some point soon after they'd left the hut, they became aware of voices. Most were muted, unintelligible, and the occasional shouts of the cartel men were calls between the scattered searchers exchanging word of their own locations.

When Ki felt the sudden rise of an upgrade under his feet, he stopped. The voices of some of the searchers were close to them now, and from their number and proximity he realized that the searchers were concentrated around the trail out of the canyon in an effort to cut off their escape.

"They're crowding around the trail up to the rim," he told Jessie and Terry in a whisper. "We'll have a better chance to get out if we go ahead one at a time."

"You've seen that trail in daylight, Ki," Jessie replied, "Terry and I haven't. Tell us where there are some landmarks we can use to find our way."

Ki said, "I've never been over it myself, Jessie. I came in by a little crack in the wall, and we've passed it. I've only seen it from a distance, from the ridge on the other side."

"We shouldn't have any trouble," Terry said. "I'll go first if you want me to and cover you and Jessie with the rifle."

"Go ahead, then," Ki said. "Jessie, you follow Terry up, and I'll be the rear guard."

Almost before Ki had finished speaking, Terry was moving off. For a moment Ki and Jessie were silent, but then she said, "I don't like to retreat, Ki, but I'm sure you know a place along the canyon rim where the three of us can stop them."

"Don't worry, Jessie. There are several places. And we

need those two rifles I cached by the trail and the ammunition in my saddlebags."

"Good. I'll follow Terry and be waiting for you."

Ki concentrated his attention on the noises coming from the canyon, but the voices he heard were so garbled that he heard nothing useful. When he judged he'd given Jessie enough of a start, he moved silently up the sloping trail until it leveled out at the rim.

On the canyon rim the darkness was more luminous. The pale light of the waning moon was already being supplemented by the first gray tinges of dawn. Ki looked around for Jessie and Terry. When he saw no sign of them, he began moving slowly along the rim. He'd taken only a few steps when Terry stepped from behind a boulder.

"I thought Jessie was coming up right behind me, Ki," he said. "Did you decide to—"

"Jessie started up here several minutes ago," Ki broke in. "You haven't seen her?"

"No. And I've been watching all the time."

"Yes, of course," Ki said. He kept his voice level, though both anxiety and anger were stabbing his mind. "Keep watching, Terry. Only one thing could've happened to her. Somebody was waiting along the trail. Jessie's been captured."

"Well, what are we waiting for?" Terry exclaimed. "They can't have gotten far! Let's go find her!"

"No," Ki said firmly. His voice was calm, but his mind was working with furious intensity. "Whoever's captured her might anticipate that both of us will go back to look for her. You stay here and keep watch. I'll go find Jessie."

Ki did not wait for Terry to reply, but turned and started back toward the canyon. He knew that whoever had taken Jessie could not be far ahead of him, and that her captor would anticipate that Ki or Terry or both would follow them back to the canyon.

Without breaking stride, Ki stepped off the trail to the rough boulder-strewn slope beside it. There were no trees or bushes for shelter, but the massive chunks of granite along the graded trail threw long dark shadows.

Ki moved with the deceptive speed of the trained *ninja* that he was, sliding from one pool of darkness to the next. In spite of his rapid progress, he advanced noiselessly, his eyes darting from side to side, all his senses focused on the terrain ahead.

His sharp vision gave Ki his first clue, and an instant later his keen hearing confirmed the half-formed image of a moving shadow ahead of him on the slopes. Almost at the same time, he heard the soft brushing of leather over stone. The hint of movement came from the base of a huge boulder that rose from the broken ground only a few paces ahead.

Since the shadow had been on his right side, Ki moved to the left with short, swift, silent steps and cut around the massive chunk of stone. He'd almost completed the circuit when he saw a ghostly movement, and then he caught a glimpse of a second wavering shadow at one edge of the first. As fleeting as the movement had been, Ki recognized the shape that had so swiftly appeared and suddenly vanished as the pointed toe of one of Jessie's boots.

Forgetting caution and silence, Ki leaped ahead and lunged past the boulder. This time he caught Jessie's captor in the full moonlight. Her mouth bound, her arms pinioned, Jessie was being carried by a man wearing a black *ninja* costume, his head covered with a mask that was a duplicate of Ki's.

Warned by the sound of Ki's sandals grinding into the soil when he braced himself to leap, the man carrying Jessie quickly let her fall to the ground. She lay motionless, and her captor whirled to face Ki. Ki did not wait for the other to attack, but he rushed ahead, swinging into a *tobi-geri* kick, its target his adversary's head.

As swift as Ki's attack had been, the mysterious *ninja* read Ki's move. Without yielding space, he stopped Ki's foot in midair with a *tegatana-uchi* block. Raising his arm to slow the foot and whirling to close the distance between them, the fake *ninja* turned, and he dropped forward into a stance in order to lash out with a *yoko-geri-keage* sideways kick that Ki evaded with a twist.

As Ki's body twirled, he saw the advantage his adversary was inadvertently offering. At the end of his twirl, Ki launched himself into a kick. Catapulting through the air, he aimed his feet at the other man's head. His feet went home and the mysterious *ninja* toppled backward, his head snapping back as he fell. The back of his head hit the base of the boulder behind him with a thudding snap as his skull crashed into its base.

Ki landed on his feet, caught his balance instantly, and hurried to Jessie's side. She was fighting her bonds. Ki slid his *tanto* out and severed them.

Jessie asked, "Who was that other *ninja,* Ki?"

"I haven't taken time to look," he told her. "I was worried about you, not him."

"I'm sure I know who he is," Jessie said, "but let's take a minute and look."

They went to the supine figure and Ki bent to strip off the man's blood-soaked hood. The twisted face staring at them with sightless eyes was that of the Count.

"I warned him not to challenge you." Schneider's guttural voice broke the silence. "But he would not listen."

Jessie and Ki came erect as they whirled. Schneider stood less than ten feet away. He was covering them with a revolver.

When neither of them replied, the cartel boss went on, "We will miss the Count, but there are others who will take his place. You should have quit while you were ahead. You should have been content to kill Bannon whom we sent to keep you occupied while we worked on taking over Tombstone. Now walk in front of me very slowly. Do not be impatient. The business we have with you will not last long. Within the hour you will both be dead."

Chapter 16

When neither Jessie nor Ki protested or even replied to his threat, Schneider grunted like an angry walrus. He motioned with a flick of his pistol, and they turned and started down the rocky slope back into the canyon. They'd gone less than half the distance to the bottom when Jessie lurched forward and almost fell. Schneider stopped short. He glanced from Ki to Jessie, who was supporting herself on her knee and bracing her torso with her hands.

"Do not play foolish games, Jessie Starbuck!" he growled. "Such childish tricks do not deceive me! I will not get near you to be attacked by your helper!"

"I'm not playing tricks!" Jessie said indignantly. "It's not easy walking over these rough rocks. Can't we move over to the trail for the rest of the way?"

"You wish to hurry to your execution, eh?" The cartel boss sneered. "Very well. It is a common custom to grant the last wish of one who is soon to die."

Motioning with his revolver for Ki and Jessie to move ahead of him, Schneider half turned as they started up the bank leading to the trail. Jessie and Ki reached the smooth surface of the trail, while Schneider was still picking his way across the rocks.

Suddenly Jessie shouted, "Schneider! Behind you!"

Startled, the cartel man turned his head to look back. The almost inaudible hiss of Ki's *shuriken* spinning through the air was drowned by two tiny pops of Jessie's little whore's gun. The *shuriken* buried itself in Schneider's jugular vein. Jessie's first bullet left a small black hole just behind the ear, and the second drilled through his jacket into his heart. Without a sound the bulky cartel boss dropped to the ground and lay still.

"I see we had the same idea," Ki said. He bent over to pick up the dead man's revolver.

"Schneider either overrated himself or underrated us," Jessie replied. "I was afraid he'd see me slip that pistol out, but obviously he didn't."

"At any rate we're rid of him," Ki went on. "But we're not through with the cartel yet, Jessie. Ritter and the others are still free."

Jessie gestured to the east, where the moon was now so pale that it was almost invisible against the brightening sky. She said, "We can deal with them in the daylight, Ki. By then we'll have three rifles and two pistols. They won't have anyone to help them plan any tricks."

"We can get the rifles at once; they're just a little way down the trail to Tombstone," Ki said. "But I'm wondering what our young friend Terry is going to say."

"I have an idea he'll still be on our side after he hears as much of our story as we can tell him," Jessie replied thoughtfully. "But let's worry about that later. Daybreak's very close now, and I'm sure Ritter and the others will be starting for Tombstone as soon as they see what's happened to their bosses."

At the top of the trail riding from the canyon floor, where it curved sharply to follow the rim, Terry Ryan stepped out of a ragged row of boulders that lined the winding path. When he saw that Jessie and Ki were moving at a slow walk, he lowered his weapon somewhat sheepishly.

"It doesn't look like you had any trouble," he said. "I've

174

been wondering what was happening down there."

"Quite a few things," Jessie replied. "Schneider and the Count are dead. Ki and I are sure that when Ritter and the rest of the gang find their bodies and discover that we've escaped as well they'll head back to town."

"You mean we're going to let them get away?"

Jessie said quickly, "Of course, we aren't going to let them get away!"

"Since we don't have any power to arrest them, we're going to jump them when they start down the trail," Ki added. "But if you don't want to get involved because you work for Governor Fremont—"

"I'm already involved, Ki," Terry said. "I've got a score to settle with that bunch, too, so I'm with you and Jessie all the way! And who says we don't have any authority to arrest them?" Seeing the puzzled look on their faces he went on, "I've got a commission in the Arizona Rangers that gives me the right to make an arrest anywhere in the territory."

Frowning, Jessie asked, "What are the Arizona Rangers, Terry? I've never heard of them."

Terry hesitated a moment then replied, "Well, right now they're just an idea of Governor Fremont's. He's thinking of organizing a force like the Texas Rangers, but he's not ready to say much about it yet. All he's done so far is to put out an executive order authorizing a skeleton force, and I've got one of the four commissions he's issued so far."

"That's all we need," Jessie said quickly. "You call on Ritter and his men to surrender, and if they don't, we'll start shooting."

"That'll suit me just fine," Terry replied. "And I'll stop Sheriff Behan from arresting you, if I have to wire the governor to back me up!"

Jessie said, "There's one thing that bothers me, Ki. Ritter

175

and the other three bosses don't deserve any mercy, but those Mexican men who work for them—well, they're just hired hands and probably don't know what they've gotten into."

"They must know something," Ki pointed out. "They were quick enough to join Ritter's bunch in chasing us last night. But you're right; they're not the ones we're after. I'd say we shouldn't make targets of them unless they shoot first."

"I wouldn't worry too much about them," Terry said. "They might not be bosses, like the other four, but I was in that canyon long enough to find out they were pretty bad eggs. If they start shooting at me, I'm sure going to shoot back!"

"Let's leave it at that, then," Jessie concluded.

"All right," Ki agreed. "Now, we'd better get busy instead of talking. It's getting lighter every minute. The rifles are just a little way ahead, and my horse is in a little clearing just a bit farther along."

With Ki leading the way, the trio walked the trail until they reached the spot where Ki had hidden the rifles. The guns were still where he'd left them, and they moved on to where he'd left his horse tethered.

As they came out of the cleft, Ki leading his mount, Jessie said, "This is a good place for one of us to hole up, Ki. I've been thinking about our ambush, and it seems to me that we ought to get Ritter's gang in a crossfire if we can."

"There are a dozen places ahead where we can hide," Ki replied. "And your crossfire is a good idea. Terry, suppose you move up the trail about fifty hards and pick out a good spot. Jessie, you can stay right here where this split gives you good cover, and I'll get on the other side of the trail between you and Terry. If Ritter takes our bait and we do our parts right, none of the gang should get away."

Before ten minutes passed, their plans for setting up the ambush had been completed and all three were in their places. They were none too soon in reaching them. Terry was still settling down when Jessie heard the thudding of hoofbeats from the direction of the canyon. Ki heard them, too, and hunkered down behind the hump he'd chosen.

The hoofbeats grew steadily louder. Ritter came in sight, his eyes fixed on the trail. Blake and Furnas were behind him, their horses shoulder to shoulder, and from their gestures the two cartel men were deep in some kind of argument. Greener slouched in his saddle staring off across the canyon, and a yard or two behind him another man was leading a horse bearing two shrouded bodies.

Jessie and Ki let the little procession pass, waiting for Terry to carry out his part of the plan. Jessie had her rifle cocked and ready, and Ki was holding a *shuriken* in each hand. Terry stepped out into the path in front of Ritter, his weapon leveled.

"You and your friends are under arrest, Ritter!" he called. "Toss your guns down on the ground and surrender!"

"It's a trap!" Ritter shouted, reaching for his revolver.

Terry was quicker than Ritter. His weapon spoke and Ritter jerked back as the slug took him. His gun sagged and the weapon dropped to the ground while the cartel man was crumpling from his saddle.

Blake and Furnas were still pulling their rifles out of their saddle holsters when Ki's first *shuriken* whirled into Blake's throat. When he saw his companion clawing at the shining star-shaped blade, Furnas tried to wheel his horse, but the trail was too narrow.

Furnas became Ki's next target, the *shuriken* driving into the base of his skull and severing his spinal cord. The cartel man leading the horse that carried the bodies leaned forward,

177

reaching for his rifle, and Jessie's slug sailed over him, but her shot was not wasted. It knocked Greener out of his saddle just as he was leveling his revolver at her. Jessie's next bullet found its mark. The unknown cartel man jerked and fell sideways to the ground.

In the sudden silence, a gentle early morning breeze began to carry away the smoke and powder fumes. The horses the cartel men had been riding were whirling and rearing, but their panic faded when there was no more shooting. By the time Ki and Jessie stepped on to the trail, the morning was quiet except for the almost inaudible whisper of the light wind.

Terry was standing in the middle of the trail, his weapon still drawn, staring at the bodies sprawled on the baked soil. Jessie started walking toward him and Ki joined her. They stopped beside Terry, who still had not moved.

Jessie said, "Stop thinking about it, Terry. It's all over now."

"I—I didn't think it'd be finished so fast," he told her. His voice was steady, but his arms were beginning to shake.

Ki said quickly, "Jessie, why don't you and Terry pick out a couple of these horses and start back for Tombstone. I'll do the cleaning up here and follow you. We'll have to report this to Sheriff Behan. I'm sure he's familiar with outlaw gangs that try to rob travelers."

Jessie understood Ki's tacit message. She dropped her voice and said, "I'll see that Terry's story matches ours, Ki."

"If I don't catch up with you on the trail, just wait for me at the sheriff's office," Ki went on. "I won't be far behind you. We should be able to answer any questions Behan might have and then get back to the hotel before these bodies draw a crowd."

"We'll ride very slowly until you catch up with us," Jessie

said. "And I'm sure that the sheriff won't hold us up with a lot of questions and formalities. After all, even if he and the governor might have some political differences, Behan's smart enough to realize that in a case of this kind, the best thing to do is to work together."

"You know, Jessie, Sheriff Behan surprised me, he was so nice about all this," Terry remarked.

"He's a shrewd politician," Jessie replied. "He knows that sometime in the future he's going to need the governor's help in solving some problem of his own."

They turned up Third Street, and when Ki saw the shops of the Chinese merchants, he said, "I'd better stop in at Quong Ki's and have a talk with him before he gets some exaggerated reports of what happened at the canyon. When do you plan for us to start back to the Circle Star, Jessie?"

"As soon as we can, Ki. Our business here is finished and we'd better get home."

"We'll be passing the OK Corral on our way to the hotel," Ki went on. "I can stop there and get seats on the carryall for tomorrow morning. Then, I'll have my visit with Quong Ki before I go on to the hotel."

"He'll probably insist that you stay and have supper with him," Jessie said. "And it wouldn't be a good idea for you to refuse him."

"Then, would you have supper with me, Jessie?" Terry asked. "We've spent a lot of time together, but there hasn't been much time for us to get better acquainted."

"Of course," she said, "I'd enjoy it."

They walked up Allen Street, Ki leaving Jessie and Terry when they reached the office of the OK Corral.

"What about the Silver Rail, Jessie?" Terry asked as they passed the saddle shop next door to the OK Corral office. "Now that Ritter's dead, won't somebody in his gang take

179

it over and keep on using it as an outlaw's headquarters?"

"I think we can leave the saloon for Sheriff Behan to worry about, Terry," she replied. "But I'm sure it won't be run by an outlaw gang any longer, now with Ritter out of the way."

At the corner of Fourth Street, Jessie nodded toward the Cosmopolitan Hotel sign and said, "I suppose this is where we separate, Terry. Ki and I are staying at the hotel across the street."

"Why, so am I," Terry said. He took Jessie's arm as they crossed the street. "At least, I suppose I am. I rented a room there when I first got to Tombstone, but only got to use it for one night."

"I'm sure it's been held for you," Jessie said as they went into the tiny lobby. She went on, "Just give me time to get the canyon dirt washed off, and change into something more presentable than this saloon girl's outfit."

"That was a very nice dinner," Jessie told Terry as they left the Maison Doree and walked the few steps to the hotel. "I feel almost civilized again."

"There was only one thing wrong with it," Terry said.

"Why, I thought it was perfect," Jessie said. "What was wrong with it?"

"We finished it too soon," he said and smiled. "I'd liked for it to last—well, a lot longer than it did. I think you're the most fascinating woman I've ever met, Jessie."

"That's a nice compliment," she replied, looking at him as they went up the stairs.

"I don't suppose you come to the Arizona Territory very often?"

"About as often as you come to Texas, I suppose." Jessie took out her key as they walked down the hall. She unlocked the door and opened it a crack. "But if you find yourself anywhere near the Circle Star, you have a standing invitation to stop in for a visit."

"Jessie—" Terry began and then stopped.

"Yes?"

"Would you mind if I kissed you good night? I guess it'll be good-bye, too, since you're leaving so early."

Without replying, Jessie tilted her head and invited Terry with her lips. What began as a brief kiss became something more as their lips clung and their tongues entwined. When they finally broke the kiss, Jessie took Terry's hand and led him into the room.

"You're right," she whispered, locking the door, "The carryall does leave early, and it would be a shame to waste the night."

"I was hoping," Terry told her, "but I wasn't sure."

He bent to find her lips again, and while their lips touched, Jessie freed the top buttons of her blouse and let it slide down to her waist. Though Terry was breathless when they finally broke the kiss, he had breath enough to gasp when he saw her full breasts. He bent and began kissing them and flicking his tongue over their tips.

For a short moment Jessie caressed his swelling shaft with her fingers before freeing it and closing her hand around its pulsing length. Moving from the door to the bed that stood across the room, inviting them, they somehow managed to help one another finish undressing.

Terry lifted Jessie off her feet and next to the bed. She spread her thighs to guide him in, then locked her ankles to draw him deeper, and held herself tightly pressed against him.

She whispered, "Now, Terry, now!"

"Of course," he replied.

Wrapping his arms tightly around her, Terry started lowering her to the bed, but Jessie's weight overbalanced him and he fell forward before they touched it. Jessie loosed a small cry of delight as the weight of his body drove him deeper into her moist depths. As he began stroking, she caught his rhythm and matched it, lifting her hips to meet his lunges.

Their delight was too great to be prolonged. The quickened gasps of Terry's warm breath brushing her cheek as the tempo of his driving increased told Jessie he was nearly at the point of release. She was more than ready after the lustiness of his stroking. When she felt Terry start trembling in his final moments, Jessie no longer held back, but let her body join his in a final frenzied shudder of completion, a gusting sigh of joy. Limp relaxation broken by small recurring spasms left her as limp and boneless as was Terry whose warm body rested on her.

They lay motionless until Jessie whispered, "Whenever you're ready again, Terry... We can sleep any time, but tonight's slipping away, and I don't want to waste a minute of it!"

Bouncing on the hard seat of the carryall as it rolled over the bumpy road to Tucson, Ki turned to Jessie and said, "I think we've broken the back of the cartel for a long time. It will be hard for them to find men to replace the leaders they've lost."

"Yes," Jessie said slowly, "this is the worst defeat we've ever been able to give them." Then she went on, a note of caution in her voice, "They'll find new leaders sooner or later, Ki. But while they're floundering around, we'll have time to rest. And whenever or wherever they pop up again, we'll be ready!"

Watch for

**LONE STAR AND THE TIMBERLAND
TERROR**

forty-third novel in the exciting
LONE STAR
series from Jove

coming in March!